A RAG,
A BONE AND A HANK
OF HAIR

Nicholas Fisk

CROWN PUBLISHERS, INC.
NEW YORK

Published in the United States in 1982
Copyright © 1980 by Nicholas Fisk
All rights reserved. No part of this publication may be reproduced,
stored in a retrieval system, or transmitted, in any form or by any means,
electronic, mechanical, photocopying, recording, or otherwise, without
prior written permission of the publisher. Inquiries should be addressed
to Crown Publishers, Inc., One Park Avenue, New York, New York 10016
Manufactured in the United States of America
Published simultaneously in Canada by General Publishing Company Limited
10 9 8 7 6 5 4 3 2 1

The text of this book is set in 12 pt. Baskerville.

Library of Congress Cataloging in Publication Data
Fisk, Nicholas.   A rag, a bone and a hank of hair.
Summary: In the twenty-third century, when children
have become scarce, an unusually bright boy is sent to live
with an experimental family of reborn 1940 Londoners.
[1. Science fiction] I. Title.
PZ7.F548Rag 1982   [Fic]   81-22192
ISBN 0-517-54635-3   AACR2

A RAG,
A BONE AND A HANK
OF HAIR

THE CHANCELLOR who led Brin through the corridors was nobody important: just an elderly man with various bits of colored ribbon on his white tunic to show how distinguished he was. Or had been. He was too old to matter now.

The corridors were long, high-arched and splendid. The tall windows were radiant and mellow with moving pictures, constantly changing, showing historical achievements of the Western world. Brin wanted to look at them carefully, but the Chancellor shuffled on anxiously, towing him along. "Quickly, young man!" he said. "They're waiting for you! The Seniors are waiting!" Brin let himself be hurried, smiling at the humped old back and the gasping voice. After all, the Chancellor was old and useless; Brin was young and priceless.

"In there boy!" said the Chancellor, and he opened the great doors. Before Brin was the Council Chamber of the Western Elect. In the chamber were the Seniors of the Western Elect. They ruled the whole Western world—one third and more of the planet Earth. They were important, but they, too, were old.

The Chancellor nervously pushed Brin toward a solitary white chair set in the middle of the curve of the Seniors' horseshoe-shaped desk. Brin made the Sign of Politeness and sat down. He did not ask permission to sit and he did not hurry as he settled himself. Comfortable, he stared at the Seniors. Silent, they stared at him.

The Chancellor—his voice shaking with respect and awe—announced Brin. "Brin Tuptal," he said, "Young Citizen First Grade, 3/HM 160—"

"We know all that," said one of the Seniors. This Senior sat in the middle: "the senior Senior," Brin said to himself. The Senior Elect. He had a long nose. He looked much older than he did on the video screens—but even on TV he looked old enough. "Let the boy speak for himself," said the Senior Elect. "Well, Brin?"

"Well," Brin replied, "I am Brin Tuptal and I'm twelve. I am cleverer than most people." He stared straight at the senior Senior, who was scratching his nose. Brin shifted his stare to a woman. She looked Indian: her hair was blue-black and her skin brown. She smiled. To her right was another Senior, a horse-faced elderly woman. She, too, smiled at Brin, showing long, white, horsey teeth.

"What is your IQ, Brin?" she asked.

"One hundred and eighty when I was tested by the Broningen rating. But it may be even higher on other ratings. I'm probably a genius."

Brin thought he heard the Senior Elect mutter, "Probably not"—but no doubt he misheard. Old people were not rude to young people.

Brin looked around him. Domed glass above him: a clear curve, showing the blue sky. It would not rain until Thursday. Today was Tuesday. He looked at the white, curved walls of the Council Chamber—the electronic displays, the illuminated moving maps, the always changing readouts. Gadgets. But there were no gadgets on the Seniors' desk. The nine Seniors made a bleak, bare picture in their white robes. Their faces supplied the only colors— one almost black, one brown, one yellow, the rest white.

"Well?" said the Senior Elect. "Go on. Don't waste time. Talk." Brin shrugged and said, "Talk about what?" He looked from face to face and began to recite, *"You* are the Senior in charge of internal social affairs. And *you,* you are the Senior in charge of food production—agriculture, fisheries, hydroponics, climate. . . ." He rolled off the words glibly, sure of himself, until the Senior Elect said, "Enough. Talk about yourself. And don't be childish."

Childish! Brin was shocked. He was seldom spoken to roughly. In Babyland, the state had taken care of him, gently. In Primary, it had been all finger painting and experiences and wonder of living. Never a cross word, never a frown. And now he was twelve, and rare, and important—and these people were being rude to him.

The horse-faced Senior interrupted his thoughts. "You were saying you were a clever person—a person of high intelligence. Tell us more, Brin." She smiled invitingly, arching her long neck to one side.

Brin said, "I knew I was different from the others. Even in Primary. They messed around and played stupid games all the time. I learned things. Lots of things."

"What sort of things?" asked the Senior with the only face Brin liked—the golden-faced Chinese-looking woman.

"Anything," Brin told her. "Everything."

She laughed. "Everything?" she said. "You learned everything?" Brin was not sure that her laughter was kind.

"I didn't mean that, you know I didn't mean that!" he said. He could hear himself getting rattled, hear his own voice rising to too high a pitch. "I don't mean that I *know* everything, just that . . ."

"Go on, go on," said the Senior Elect. Other Seniors were smiling privately. Brin was confused. He was not used to being laughed at. Sulkily, he refused to speak.

At last the Chinese Senior said, "So you learn very fast, do you?"

"Very fast indeed. Faster than anyone I know. Faster than anyone in the Teens. I'm twelve, but they've put me in with the Teens because I know so much. I'm brilliant, they say I'm brilliant. I can learn anything—"

"Oh dear, oh dear, he won't do," said the Senior Elect. "Swellheaded little ape," he seemed to mutter. (But that, Brin knew, was impossible. No one dared be that rude to a young person.) The black Senior yawned. The horse-faced Senior looked over Brin's head.

"What's politics? What's ecology? Quick!" snapped the black-faced Senior.

Brin jumped. "P-politics," he began, hearing himself stutter, "is the art and science of ruling people—of ruling *peoples*—"

"Well, well," sneered the Senior elect. "Try ecology."

"Ecology is the science of preserving the place we live in—taking care of the environment and—"

The Senior Elect cut him short "What are *Reborns?*" he demanded.

Brin gaped at him. He wasn't sure he had heard right. Had he really said *"Reborns"*?

"Reborns, Reborns, *Reborns!*" said the Senior, leaning over the table. "Tell us about them!"

"But they mustn't be talked about!"

"Oh yes they must. Here and now. Quickly!"

"Reborns are manufactured people," Brin began. "New people made out of old people."

"How?" asked the Senior Elect.

"There could be several ways, I don't know if—"

"You told us a moment ago that you'd learned everything," said a youngish Senior, a woman, who had not spoken before. She had big eyes and a tight little mouth, but now it was open, showing small white teeth. The round eyes were staring at him. He was not used to being stared at.

Brin sat back in his chair, feeling his back meet the soft pad. He settled himself deliberately: braced his mind and body and said, "You're all rude and stupid. You are the Seniors, but you behave like bad children. I'd like to go now."

"That's better!" said the Senior Elect, rubbing his narrow hands and smiling. "Go on, boy. Tell us about Reborns."

"Only if you obey the Rules of Politeness," said Brin, making the Sign of Politeness used by all Westerners when a discussion goes wrong and a quarrel might start—a touch of the fingers to the head, where the brain is; then to the heart. It was an old sign, an ancient sign. The Christians had used something like it until a few centuries ago.

Most of the Seniors made the sign back, but two of them didn't. Brin got to his feet and prepared to leave.

The voice of the Senior Elect stopped him. The voice was gentle now. "Please sit down, Brin." The Senior made the sign, and Brin automatically replied. "Tell us about the Reborns. Tell us what you know and don't know. We are on a friendly footing now—"

"We had to test you," said the golden-faced woman. "We have to find out if you are the right person to do the work we want done. But tell us about Reborns." She smiled. Her face was charming.

Brin settled back in his chair and began.

"First," he said, "I will tell you what I know—what people are saying, that is. Because we don't really know anything, only what you let us know. Anyhow . . .

"In the last century, there was an accident at the Euronuclear power plant. A leakage. After the accident, the birthrate began to fall. Many people who wanted to be parents could not have children. Children became very—very valuable, because there weren't enough of them. Of us. So we had to be taken care of. Educated carefully, brought up to be healthy and so on.

"Then," he continued, "the damage proved worse than anyone thought. The accident affected the whole world. There were fewer and fewer children. So the population of the world kept decreasing. And those stupid jokes started—you know, 'Robots Rule!'—all those jokes about the machines taking over our world when all the people were gone."

" 'Robots Rule!' " said one of the Seniors. "Very good!" The Senior Elect waved him silent and said, "Go on, Brin."

"Well, there had to be more people, far too few could be born naturally. So you Seniors started thinking about Reborns. And now everyone has heard rumors about them, but nobody really knows what they'll be like, or what they are, or will be."

"Do you know?" a Senior asked.

"I've read about it. Genetics, DNA, genes, chromosomes, the elements of living things—"

"How do you think Reborns will be made?"

"Every part of every living thing," Brin began, "contains its own recipe. A tiny bit of lettuce contains the recipe for the whole lettuce. Part of a fingernail contains the recipe for the whole fingernail. Scraps of bone and tissue from the flesh of a cat or dog contain the recipe for the whole animal—"

"Very well put!" said the Chinese Senior, beaming.

"Excellent!" agreed the Senior Elect. "Go on."

Brin continued, "I suppose what you'd do is something like this: you'd get various scraps of tissue, bone, anything, and put them in a genetic recoder. And then in a sort of soup. With some electricity, of course. You'd cook it up. And then you would have living matter, even a living human being. A new human just the same as the old one. A reborn human."

"Right!" said the black Senior. "Right, that is, in every way, but one. You said, 'That is what we would do.' You should have said, 'That is what we have done!' "

Brin said, "You mean, the rumors are true? You have already made some Reborns?"

"Yes. Otherwise we would not have encouraged the rumors."

"Are there many Reborns?"

"No—very, very few."

"Are they—all right? Do they behave like real human beings?"

"They *are* real human beings. Not robots, or machines, or androids, or those delightful creatures in the old films—"

"You mean Frankenstein's monsters?" Brin said. "With

nuts and bolts sticking out of their necks and great big boots on?"

To Brin's astonishment, the Senior Elect began to chuckle. "Well, well! Remarkable boy! Seen everything, knows everything. Even the ancient motion pictures! Mind you, I never understood what the heavy boots were for. Slippers far more suitable—"

Brin grew impatient and interrupted. "So you have solved the problem of repeopling the planet?" he said.

"Ah," said the Indian Senior. She stroked her chin and stared at Brin.

"Ah," said the other Seniors, looking at Brin and one another.

There was a silence until the black Senior said, "There are problems. Problems . . ." The dark eyes in the broad, powerful face fixed themselves on Brin's eyes: "But you are going to solve them, Brin!"

"This way," said the black Senior, putting his heavy hand on Brin's shoulder and guiding him through a door in a long, bare corridor.

There was a guard at the door, a hard-faced woman in the usual one-piece uniform made of Adamant. Brin could see her determined face through the visor of her helmet and almost hear the whispering of her uniform's air-conditioning unit. Adamant let nothing in—and nothing out, so the unit had to do her body's breathing. *Fsss!* went the aircon unit, and each time Brin smelled the awful perfume the woman wore.

The black Senior said, "Brin, you ought to know my

name. I am Tello, after Othello. Do you know who Othello was?"

Brin promptly answered, "Othello, Moorish general—Moors were black. William Shakespeare tragedy, still performed—"

Tello chuckled and held up a big hand to silence Brin. "All right," he said. "You know about Othello."

The guard said "Prints, please."

"You know me, Maisie!" Tello turned to the guard, laughing.

"I know I want your prints. Yours and his."

"The boy hasn't got prints, he's just a—a boy—"

"Get away from here, then. You and the boy. Come back when you've got prints." She put her hand on the Viper control on her belt. Tello backed away, laughing and protesting. "All right, Maisie! We'll go quietly! Won't come back until we both have prints!" They walked down the corridor, away from the door. Tello shook his head and smiled. "She's a dragon, that one!"

"But she was rude! Almost violent!" Brin said.

"Trained to be," Tello said, contentedly.

"But I thought the whole *idea* of our society was . . ." Brin began, then gave up.

"Sweetness and light?" Tello said. "No violence, no aggression?" He chuckled. "Well, that's what you see. And Maisie is what you don't see. But she's there all the same."

"But she wouldn't have hurt you, would she?"

"Not me! Perhaps you. Though she has known me for years, she'd have had you smoking on the floor if we hadn't left!"

"Smoking?"

"When you get hit by a Viper, you burn. When you burn, you smoke."

"What *is* a Viper?"

"The weapon in the suit. The weapon is the suit, and the suit is the weapon. Maisie just occupies the weapon. She doesn't have to be strong—just strong-minded. And Maisie's that!"

Now they were in what seemed to be a records office. The man behind the desk took Brin's hand and did things with it over bits of plastic and a little machine that hummed.

Brin paid no attention. He guessed, correctly, that the fingermarks were being recorded and registered and when this was done he could put his prints on the coding panel of the door Maisie guarded. Then the door would be opened for him. He wondered what could be behind the door.

Something very important. Something as important as a Reborn? He could not ask such questions out loud, so he kept still while the man behind the desk fussed about with computers and card machines and all the rest of it.

"Completed, sir," the man said to Tello. ("Sir!" thought Brin. He had never heard the word used except in old films and TV programs.)

Now the man was speaking to him. "This is your card, sir." ("Me a 'sir'!" thought Brin.) "You'll need to write down your code number—"

"I don't need to. I can remember it. I can remember any number you like—"

"Write it down, sir. Then sign your name underneath in your usual handwriting. Thank you. That is all."

"Don't I get the card?"

"Certainly not! We keep the card, sir."

"What does all of this mean?" asked Brin. "Does it mean I can go in anywhere—into all the doors in this place, past all the guards?"

"Oh no, sir. Nothing like that, sir. It means that you can print in—you may enter certain places—in the company of a Senior. But only when accompanied by a Senior."

"What nonsense!" said Brin. "I thought all this sort of thing had been done away with centuries ago!"

"Did you, sir?" said the man. "Did you think that?" Coolly he turned away and went back to his machines.

"Come on, boy," said Tello. He began chuckling again as they walked back along the corridor. "He's got a card. He's got coded status, and a number, and he can actually *print in*—and he's grumbling!"

Brin, confused, said nothing.

At the guarded door, Maisie said, "Prints, please."

Tello put out his hand, first to a flat plate on Maisie's shoulder, then to a similar plate to the side of the door. A rose-pink light in the door lit and slowly faded.

"Now the boy."

Brin imitated Tello's actions. Again the rose-pink light glowed and faded. The door opened.

They entered a small room. It had another door that was closed. They sat down. Tello was silent now and unsmiling. Brin fidgeted and at last said, "Where am I going? What's going to happen?"

The second door opened and a pretty girl said, "Tello, sir. And Brin. Please come in."

They walked straight into November 1940.

November 1940 was badly lit, smelly, spacious, complicated, clumsy, dingy and noisy. The noises were small. A ticking clock, a dripping faucet, a kitchen stove whose grate went *"Grr-grr-tang!"* as the live coals dropped under the vibration of their footsteps, then gently clicked and murmured as the coals settled and burned anew.

"The 1940 Scenario, sir," said the pretty girl, smiling brightly.

"The what?" said Brin. Only half of what he saw meant anything to him. That over there—that was obviously a chair of some kind, but what kind? The girl, following his eyes, said, "Wicker chair. Wicker is sort of sticks, things that grow. People collected them, twisted them, made them into chairs and so on." She went to the chair and sat down. Her neat trouser suit looked garish against the creaking yellowish wicker and faded floral cushion of the chair.

Tello said, "Give him the guided tour, Madi."

"Wouldn't you rather? I mean, you are in charge . . . ?"

"You did the work. Tell him all about it."

The girl called Madi said, "Right. Do I call you Brin or sir?"

"Brin."

"Well, Brin, this is the kitchen pantry and scullery of an old house in West London of 1940. There is an outhouse through that door, the 'back door.' You are standing in the kitchen. Facing the window, on that wall, you can see a dresser, with drawers and shelves to hold the plates and knives and forks and other things for cooking and serving food. That thing you are looking at shouldn't be on the dresser, it should be in one of the drawers. It's called an eggbeater, and it works like this." She took hold of the gray and silver implement and whirled its handle.

"It could actually work!" said Brin. "You could beat eggs with that thing!"

"It did work," the girl said, putting it in a dresser drawer. "It does work! Definitely beats eggs!" She smiled briefly at Brin and picked up the next exhibit, the clock. "Alarm clock!" she announced, shaking it. It made faint tinny noises, then it started ticking again, tick-tock, tick-tock. "Tells the time," said Madi, "rings a bell to wake you up or get the food out of the oven when it's done. Okay?"

"What oven?" said Brin, still amazed, but fascinated.

She showed him the cast-iron stove and an ugly gray and white gas one, with brass taps. She showed him rolling pins and jelly molds, cans of dessert powder and a safe for meat made of wood and galvanized metal; flypapers and crackers, shoe polish and scouring powder, coal and gelatin, mousetraps and irons.

Brin drank it all in.

"You see, the scullery is where you take the dirty things

to be washed—there's the sink, there's the sink tidy, and the little mop and brush for the dishes, and soap powder—Brin, are you sure you are remembering all this?"

"I'm sure," he said.

"That's why we picked him," said Tello, smiling happily from the creaking wicker chair.

"I don't trust him!" The girl laughed. "What's a Ewbank, Brin?"

He said, "Carpet sweeper. That wood-cased thing with rubber wheels and brushes inside."

"Hoover?"

"Vacuum cleaner. Kept in that closet over there."

"Skipper?"

"Sardines."

"Main?"

"The name on that gas stove."

"Cherry Blossom?"

"Boot polish. But they wear shoes, not boots."

The girl paused. "He's good, sir," she said to Tello. "You picked the right boy! Now listen carefully. There's a lot to remember . . ."

Later she questioned Brin. "What is blancmange? Methylated spirits? Stair rod? Icebox? Lard? What's the difference between socks and stockings? Between coal and coke? Between shoes and slippers?"

Brin got every answer right. When she said, "November 1940 . . . what is happening in the world?" he answered, "World War II has started in Europe and. . . ." He told her at length.

"You're marvelous, Brin!" said.

"No I'm not. I can't answer some questions."

"What questions?"

Brin put his hands on his hips, stared her in the face and said, "Why am I here? What's it all for? What's a scenario?"

"Ah," said Tello, "I'll answer, Madi. . . ."

"First," Tello said, when Brin was sitting uncomfortably on a hard wooden kitchen chair covered with chipped cream paint, "First, the word *scenario.*

"A scenario is a setting for people, or actions, or both. It's like a stage set—but also like a situation. Now, we need both. We need a *place* for certain characters to act out their play; we also need a *situation* in which those people will feel at home."

"What people? What characters?"

"Come to that in a moment. You asked. 'Why am I here?' You're here because you are the right age and because you have a wonderful memory and an ability to learn fast. You are here because you're probably the only person who could do the job.

"You asked," he continued, " 'What's it all for?' Well, that's easily answered. It's here for the Reborns."

"The Reborns!"

"That's what I said. The Reborns. They are the central characters in the play. This scenario was lovingly put together by Madi for them. All these things—these wicker chairs and mousetraps and kitchen sinks and I-don't-know-whats—Madi had them reborn, found them, or had them made. Are you beginning to understand?"

Brin thought, and said, "Of course! Yes! I see it! The Reborns are 1940 people, you've picked people from that period—and this is their home, the place where they'll feel at home—"

"That's it," said Tello, smiling and leaning back in his creaky chair.

"But why bother with this scenario? Why not bring them straight into our own time? Why go back in the past?"

Before Tello could answer, Brin said, "No—wait—the past: why go back to the past for Reborns? Why go to all that trouble? Why not make reborns from *proper* people— recently dead people of our own time? Why go back to 1940?"

"Uh-uh!" said Tello. Think, Brin! You're not thinking! Think!"

Brin thought. At last he said, "Oh. I see. I get it."

"What do you get?"

"Well, it's a sort of catch, isn't it? Catch question, catch answer. We need Reborns because our people, the *real* people, can't reproduce themselves anymore. And if you made Reborns from Reborns, you'd only produce *more* people who couldn't breed—which would mean producing more Reborns. In fact, you'd be stuck with Reborns for the whole future of mankind!"

"You've got it," Tello said. "But I ask you again—why 1940? Why not 1920, 1960, 1980? Why 1940 in particular?"

"The war?" Brin said. "Has that got something to do with it?"

"Go on," Tello said.

"The war . . ." Brin muttered. "Let me think. . . . There was the blackout. And fear of bombs. And rationing and shortages—"

"Good boy!" Tello said. "More."

"Well, I suppose people led restricted lives. Almost like being in prison. You were stuck in your home, once darkness fell, because there was no point in going out."

"And there was no point in *wanting* to go out," Tello said, continuing Brin's thought. "Go out for what? For a meal? Well, you could, but restaurant meals weren't very good. And children didn't go by themselves to restaurants. The movies? Yes—but buses and trains stopped early, and there was the blackout to consider and children weren't allowed into movies without an accompanying adult. So people stayed home. They expected to stay home. Which suits our scenario nicely."

"But you could have used a later period?" Brin asked.

"Perhaps. But probably not. By 1960 or 1980, children wanted all kinds of things—and got what they wanted! They expected freedoms and possessions and excitements. So later children wouldn't have done for us. They would have become impatient with the scenario. We could condition our Reborns not to become impatient—but that wouldn't do either. Too much conditioning tampers with the natural being we want to observe."

Brin interrupted. "All right. But why bother with this scenario? Why not bring the 1940 Reborns right into our own time, straight away?"

Tello said, "Look, we can't drag people out of their graves and put them in a completely new place and situation! They must be put at ease. Otherwise they might be terrified, angry, shocked, anything. And worse than that—"

"Worse than that, we wouldn't be able to understand *them?*" Brin suggested.

"Right!" said Tello. "We don't want to know what our Reborns might do or should do or could do. We want to know what they *do* do—how they behave in their own surroundings, living life their own way. Only then can we find how to bring them 'up to date'—how to help them fit in with our times, our lives. How to find them a place, if there *is* a place for them. Perhaps there isn't. Perhaps the jump from then to now is too much for anyone to make. We must find out. When we've learned all we need to learn about them, we can try different ways, perhaps. We can throw them in at the deep end, try mixing Reborns of different races and periods, try anything. But not at first. . . ."

"And where," Brin said, "do I come in?"

"Oh, didn't I tell you?" Tello said. "The first Reborns were young people. People of your age or younger. People not too old to learn. We have had failures and successes. . . ."

Brin scratched his left armpit. "So," he said.

"So you're it!" Tello beamed. "You're the host! You're the one who's going to live with them, share their lives, learn about them!"

Brin got up from the chair so fast that it fell over backward. "I'm not, you know!" he said. "I'm going straight back home to my own life, with my own friends! I'll live in my own time and learn the things I want to learn!"

Tello smiled more broadly than ever and said, "You'll do as you're told, boy." Madi picked up the fallen chair and gently pushed Brin's shoulders until he sat in it. "We all have a duty, Brin," she said, smiling prettily at him. "We have to do our duty."

"I won't do mine," Brin said.

Tello stood up. "Don't be silly," he said, in his velvety bass. "I told you: you're *it*. And when one of the Seniors tells you a thing like that, you just simply say, 'Yes, sir.' " The big, dark face was still smiling, still pleasant, still likable. But Brin could also see something else in it, something hard as rock—something that made Tello a Senior and himself a Junior.

"Yes, sir . . . ?" Tello prompted.

"I suppose so," Brin muttered. "Yes, sir."

The ugly old alarm clock on the dresser went *brrrrrr!* and Madi said, "You've got a quarter of an hour, Brin. Thee's a lot to learn in that time."

"And at the end of that time?" Brin asked, miserably.

"They arrive," Madi said.

It took Brin only ten minutes to learn all he needed to know: to find out about knife sharpeners, can openers, ink, dish mops, drain boards, breadboxes, coffee percolators, the importance of cups of tea and the cat's bowl of milk.

And to change into his 1940 clothes—long itchy socks, heavy shoes, flannel pants, a shirt and a stupid thing called a tie. He kept his own underwear.

He had plenty of time to ask the questions that really interested him. "Is this all there was, Madi? Just these rooms?"

"No. This is just a part of a house of that period. Many people in those days lived in big houses with lots of rooms. Above this set of rooms there should be other rooms—bedrooms, bathrooms, an attic. Next to it, there'd be a dining room and a sitting room. There's a garden outside—you can see a little bit of it through the window."

"But the Reborns will want to go to those other rooms."

"No they won't. We made the Reborns. We programed them—conditioned them to expect and accept what we offer them."

"But couldn't you have offered them a bit more than this?" Brin asked, looking around the dingy room.

Madi rolled her eyes. "If you knew the trouble, the effort, the research, that went into getting just this bit done! That carpet over there—that little thing in front of the stove—that's a Reborn! It's made of cotton and wool, natural fibers; we had to reborn it from a little old tuft we found—"

"But what about the other things?"

"We had to find them. Or make them. And that's not all. We had to 'antique' them—give the appearance of being old and used. That aluminum coffee percolator, all stained at the bottom—"

"It's incredible!"

"Incredible. Yet nothing compared with making the Reborns themselves."

"Tell me about making them," Brin said.

"There's no time. And even if there was, I don't know enough. I'm just an effects worker, I have nothing to do with the people side. And the people will be here any minute now."

"I wish you'd tell me more about them."

"There's Mavis, nine. And Brian, eleven. Brother and sister. Wait and see."

"You could at least tell me if they're bigger or smaller than me—if they're clever or stupid—if—"

Madi put a finger to her lips, swung the whole dresser outward like a great door, stepped behind it and swung the dresser shut.

Brin caught her whispered words. "They're here! Ready?"

"I suppose so," Brin muttered.

The door opened and Mavis and Brian came in.

Mavis called, "Coooee," then stopped short, hand to mouth, when she saw Brin. "Oh! I'd forgotten about you!" she said.

She held out her right hand. Brin took it and shook it. He looked at her eagerly, inspecting her, but she did not meet his eyes. She just shook his hand, limply, and said, "I'm Mavis. Well, you know that. . . . Brian, Brin's here!" Then, remembering her manners, she said, "How do you do," and looked him in the eye for the first time.

She was as tall as Brin although she was only nine. Her head seemed small to Brin, but well-shaped and rather pretty. Her hair, cut short, was not quite clean, and it was held in place with—what was the word?—a barrette, a little imitation-tortoiseshell clip. She saw him staring at it and her ink-stained fingers flew to it and unclipped it. "School rule, we have to wear them!" she said and then grinned awkwardly.

Brian came in.

To Brin, he looked like an animal. His knees were gray with dirt, red with a cut, white where the skin had been scraped. One of his teeth was crooked. There was ink on one ear. He put out his strong, dirty hand.

"I'm Brian. How do you do?" he said. He stared at Brin, with his mouth half open in an awkward grin. Brin saw bits of metal in Brian's back teeth. Fillers? No, fillings.

Brin realized he was being rude by looking so openly at Brian. You were supposed to be shy, it was bad manners to stare. He wondered whether he should say something. He began to say, "How do you—" when Brian leaped away from him and shouted, "Bananas!" He grabbed a banana, peeled it and then stopped. "Gosh," he said. "There's only two. Do you want one, Brin?"

Mavis said, "Ladies first, thank you!" and took the banana from her brother. She began to eat it.

"Well, how do you like that!" Brian exploded.

Brin said, "I don't want a banana. You have the other one."

Brian said, "We could split it." He paused, then said, *"Banana split, get it? Ho, ho!"*

Brin did not know what he meant but he laughed anyway. Mavis, her banana nearly finished, imitated her brother's laugh.

"No need to get smart," Brian said angrily.

"Well, I *mean*," Mavis said scornfully. "You and your ho, ho, ho! Is that all they teach you in school?"

"Stop it!" Brian said, and stuffed the banana into his mouth, scowling.

Brin watched and listened. The sky was turning gray. Mavis flicked the switch by the door and the room suddenly blazed with a harsh light. Every ugly detail was revealed.

Brin looked and despaired.

Yet half an hour later, he was happy.

The happiness began when Brian had kicked his book bag into the corner, loosened his school tie, thrown his cap at the dresser and made himself comfortable. He said, "Let's have soldier's toast! With Marmite!"

Brian and Mavis crouched by the kitchen stove holding buttered bread over the glowing coals until the underside scorched. Brin watched amazed. The half-burned bread and butter was smeared with brown stuff from a little dark pot with a paper label on it showing a picture of a different little brown pot: this was obviously Marmite.

Mavis said, "Here you are, Brin! More in a sec!" and pushed the burned, smeared bread at him on a long wire fork. He wondered what to do with it. He waited until Mavis and Brian did something.

It *was* food: they ate it.

He took a tiny bit. Then a larger bite. Then an enormous bite.

Salty, buttery, crunchy yet soft. Delicious!

"Encore!" Brian said.

"Encore!" said Brin, hoping the word would mean another piece.

It did. And a third, this time with tea from a brown pot.

"Super!" Brin said, and he meant it.

"What did you think of your first day?" Madi asked. She had a squeaker on a gold chain around her neck, so Brin knew that their conversation was being recorded. Later, the little squeaker, no bigger than a brooch, would be slotted into a scripta. The tiny wire spool inside would squeak its record of the conversation. The scripta would turn sounds into written words for microfilm projection, so that the words could be read; or for coding and filing in the Memory Bank; or anything else.

Squeakers were among the few things that made Brin nervous. He hated to say—and have recorded—anything foolish or imprecise. He knew that his squeaker record would be studied by the Seniors. So he answered Madi grudgingly and carefully. "It was okay," he said.

"Okay?" Madi smiled brightly at him, demanding more.

"Okay. But difficult. They speak a different language. They never say what they mean. They sort of . . . make a sketch of their thoughts and intentions. They hide everything behind catchphrases and acting. They are not like us."

"I know what you mean," Madi said. "I was watching and listening. Go on."

"Well, it's hard to know what they're really thinking, what they're really like," Brin said, lamely.

"I know. I've made a list of some of their words and phrases." She squeezed the squeaker to change track. Its little voice squeaked, *"Bats. Nuts. Super. Gosh. I say. Dopey. Crazy. Gotcha."* It sang, in a mocking voice, *"The roses round the door . . . make me love Mother more"* (Brian sang that when Mavis had said something "dopey"). It sang, *"I Like a Nice Cup of Tea in the Morning"* (that was when Mavis put the kettle on). It repeated, *"How do you do. Thank your mother for the rabbit."*

"What do you make of all that, Brin?"

"I don't know. Catchphrases. From the radio. They have it on a lot, in the background."

"They had records, too." she said. "No, television, of course. But they did have movies. So Mavis and Brian were quoting what they heard on the radio and on records."

"But why do they never seem to speak any of their own thoughts?" asked Brin.

"Perhaps they are shy. Perhaps they hide behind the catchphrases."

"Oh perhaps," Brin said, "they have nothing to say. Nothing worth saying. . . ."

After a pause, Madi said, "Does that mean you don't think very much of them?"

"I don't know," Brin said. "You shouldn't ask that after just one meeting. It's too early to tell."

"But we've got to find out as quickly as possible. I'm sure you know why."

"Well, it's obvious. We've got to know whether people of this quality are worthwhile. Whether the breed is good enough—"

" 'Silk purse, sow's ear,' " Madi said. "We've got to know which."

"Well, I don't know which. It's too early to say."

"Are they as intelligent as you?" Madi asked.

"No."

"Are they as well educated as you?"

"No. How could they be? They belong to the old days. Nearly three centuries ago. The days following the first industrial revolution. They didn't have computers or robots or a controlled climate or Sleepers or anything. . . ."

He broke off and thought about Sleepers. Sleepers educated you when you were asleep. The surgeon put the Sleeper in the baby just after it was born. The Sleeper monitored and fed the mind, intelligence, health and behavior of the infant-child-adolescent-adult. It made a human a successful, social, civilized being. Mavis and Brian did not have Sleepers. They were merely conditioned. Brin had a Sleeper in him like everyone else: just there, inside, at the back of his skull on the right. He touched the place.

"Why are you thinking about your Sleeper?" asked Madi.

"I don't know. I suppose because they—Mavis and

Brian, all those people from the time before the accident—didn't have them. They must have been very different from us, completely different. Perhaps so different that we can never really come to terms with them—"

"Never *use* them? As Reborns? Is that what you mean?"

"Well, they had *wars*, didn't they? Mavis and Brian—their scenario is set at the beginning of a *world war!* Only criminals wage war."

"Quite so," Madi said. "What differences have you observed?"

"They're a bit heavier, and taller. A bit coarser. And—their heads might be smaller."

"Coarser?" asked Madi.

"Well, that could just be an impression. I mean, the clothes they wear, the things they use—they're coarse things. Things that make dirt, like the ink pens they used to write with, or the coal fire, or having to use your hands so much to do things. They even cook things themselves!"

"But you liked the toast?"

"Very much."

"What could be coarser than that?" Madi demanded.

"I liked it very much," Brin repeated. "That's what I mean. Just because something is coarse, it doesn't mean it's bad. Or does it? I don't know. *You* don't know."

"But the absence of Sleepers?" Madi said.

"Oh, that's different. That must make a great difference. But I don't know *what* difference. How can I know?"

"Violence?" said Madi, softly. "Aren't you afraid of that? Aren't you afraid that, at any moment, you might have to face violence from Mavis or Brian—or both?"

"Violence?" Brin said, staring at her. "But that means breaking the First Law!" He stopped short and laughed uneasily. "I see what you mean," he said. "It was Sleepers that made the First Law work. Sleepers stop us from being violent. Any of us. And that's why the world has—just gone on, without wars and violent crimes and murders and all that. . . ."

"Sleepers were not invented until 2040," Madi reminded him. "And they were not used, all over the world, until 2070. So Mavis and Brian—"

"You've put me in a jungle!" Brin said. His voice shook. "You've put me among people who could turn out to be violent! People without Sleepers! Why didn't I think? Why did I let you do it? I'm not going back, I'm not—!"

Madi just laughed. "You'll be all right, Brin. I'm right there behind the dresser, remember? As for murder and violence and all the rest of it—that was rare even in those days. Ordinary people didn't often hurt or kill each other."

"They did! And not just one at a time! Millions at a time in the war!"

She laughed. Brin began to feel foolish, then wondered how good Madi would be in dealing with violence. Probably very good. She seemed to be good at everything.

"Mrs. Mossop enters the scenario this evening," Madi reminded him. "You'd better change back into your 1940 clothes and get ready."

He made a face and changed his clothes.

———

He heard Mrs. Mossop in the kitchen before he saw her. She was singing. Under her singing, there was a constant dull thumping noise. She sang:

> *"I'll cook some bacon,*
> *I'll cook some bacon,*
> *I'll cook some bacon for my tea."*

Then there was an unusually loud bump and Brin heard her mutter, "Damn the devil!" and make grumbling noises. He stood outside the kitchen door wondering what she would be like. He recognized the song. It was Mrs. Mossop's version of "La Cucaracha," a song popular in 1940—often played on the radio.

Now Mrs. Mossop was singing "Red Sails in the Sunset" in her high, vague voice. The thumping had started again. He drew a deep breath and opened the door leading into the kitchen; on his side of the door was a sort of noplace called "the passage." He went into the kitchen, leaving his own century behind.

Mrs. Mossop looked up from her ironing and, with no surprise in her voice, said, "You'll be him, then, Master Brin. Well, I never. All the way from the Bahamas."

Brin said, "How do you do, Mrs. Mossop." She replied, "Well, I never," sniffed, and went on ironing.

There seemed nothing for Brin to say or do, so he watched her. She had two old-fashioned irons, one in her hand with a padded cloth around its handle and the other heating up in front of the stove. The thumping noise was made by the iron in use as she brought it down, *thump,* on her work. Her hands were red and veined. The special electric light over the table, turned on only when Mrs. Mossop ironed, lit her forearms and face. Her bare arms and face were tanned. When the iron went thump, her chin and cheeks quivered and sometimes her small gold-rimmed glasses wobbled over her short, shining nose.

At last Brin asked, "Haven't you got an electric iron?" She said, "I don't like them, Master Brin," and began to sing a song about a chapel in the moonlight. "Oh, I love to 'ear the organ," she sang, then went to the stove to change irons. "When we're strolling down the aisle," she sang to herself, "where roses entwine." Brin wondered what an aisle was and what he should say next, if anything.

She said, "The Bahamas, is it? Well, I never. Where might they be when they're at home?"

He told her about his life in the Bahamas. It had been decided that the Bahamas were a good place for Brin to have come from: a long way from Britain, but British. Nobody would want to question too closely. Everyone would assume that his strangeness was due to coming from a strange, distant place.

Mrs. Mossop hardly listened to him. She began to sing again under her breath. Once or twice she said, "Fancy that," or "Well I never," to keep him talking. When the iron went cold she said, "Damn the devil," and changed it for the hot one.

He stopped talking and studied her face: the little mouth, pursed with effort; the heavy, worn, solid flesh; the lines around her eyes. Looking at her was like—like what? Like looking at a tree, he decided: something strong, unlikely to change, simple yet complicated. Something sure of itself. Looking at her was not like looking at a stranger. Like a tree, she was something he felt he had always known.

"Damn that cat!" she said. Blackie—Brin had never seen it before—had leaped up on the pile of ironing. "Cats never change," thought Brin. "Go away! Shoo!" Mrs. Mossop said, threatening the cat with the hot iron. The cat pushed its nose forward to smell and feel the heat—pulled its head back disdainfully—then curled itself on the warm ironing and blinked its eyes at Mrs. Mossop.

"That's his lordship for you," Mrs. Mossop said. "Black devil! Ought to be made into tennis rackets!" Brin did not know what she meant: didn't know that, in the old days, rackets were strung with "catgut." He noticed that Mrs. Mossop made a new place for her completed ironing to allow room for Blackie. "Tea for two and two for tea," she sang. "None for you, and all for me." To the cat she said, "Imp of Satan!" It purred.

"Staying here, then, are you?" she said to Brin a little later.

"Just till my uncle comes over," he told her.

The uncle was part of the Bahamas story. He was a Royal Air Force scientist (this might help account for Brin's brightness, and "scientist" was a vague word anyway).

"Oh well, you'll be safe here until Hitler starts up. If he

does. Then it will be back to the Bahamas for you, double quick. . . ." She wiped her brow with her arm. "I just do the ironing and help out," she said. "But *you'll* be safe, I dare say."

Brin knew enough by now to understand that she was talking for the sake of talking. Her words had no particular meaning. She said things that needed no answer. He wished Mrs. Mossop would say real things, interesting things. He wished she would tell him about herself and her life, her feelings and likes and dislikes. But he knew instinctively that she would not.

She cut across his thoughts by saying, "Well, look at the clock!" He looked at it and saw nothing remarkable. "Teatime!" she said and smiled for the first time. Her teeth were white and regular—obviously false. "You fill the kettle, Master Brin." To the cat she said, "Get off, Hitler!" She piled up the ironing while he filled the kettle from the brass faucet in the cold scullery, thinking, "So far, she's called the cat Hitler, his lordship and imp of Satan."

"I like my cup of tea," she said to him, earnestly, rattling cups on saucers at great speed. "But none of your dishwater. Give us that tea caddy. . . ."

"I like soldier's toast," Brin said, watching her put five spoonfuls of tea in the pot. "We don't have that in the Bahamas."

"You don't want none of that," she told him. "You want crumpets. You look in that bag and you'll find crumpets from Osgoods. Fresh from Osgoods."

Crumpets? He looked in her patchwork-leather bag for something that could be crumpets, but there were so many things, so many packages and bags. He pulled out a large white bag with something spongy and soft in it, but he didn't think it could be crumpets, so he went on looking. At last he had to say, "I'm sorry, but I can't find them."

"Can't find them? You're holding them in your hand!"

"These? These are crumpets?"

"Lord bless us and keep us—of course. Give 'em over!" She reached out her hand for the bag, impatiently. Then her face softened. "Ah, but I dare say you've never seen a crumpet? Oh well, a foreigner, that accounts for it. Never had crumpets!"

There was pity in her voice.

"Well?" said Madi. Senior Tello was there also asking questions.

"Well, it's all going . . . well," Brin said uncertainly.

"What's puzzling you?" asked Tello.

"Nothing, everything." Suddenly angry, Brin said, "It's okay for you, you're just watching and recording everything. But I'm in there, with them."

"That's why your impressions matter more than anyone else's" Tello said. "We need your descriptions, feelings, opinions—everything. Tell us about today." He settled back expectantly.

Brin's mind was a jumble. "I understand everything about them except what they're really like," he said.

"Well," Madi prompted, "are they primitives? Savages?"

"No, of course not! Obviously not! It's just that—that they're so different from us."

"Tell us about today," Tello repeated. "Tell it like a story."

Brin did his best.

"That Hitler," Mrs. Mossop had said, "Ought to be sliced small. Hanging's too good for him! Put him through the grinder, that's what I'd do. . . ."

"Kick him in the stomach!" Brian suggested, cheerfully.

"Use his guts for garters!" Mrs. Mossop said.

"Give him the Chinese water torture!" Mavis said, clasping her arms around her knees. "They fill you up with water," she continued, "more and more water. Through a funnel. Until you actually burst!"

"Burst?" said Brian. "You'd never burst!"

"They do," Mavis said primly. "I know they do."

Brin had felt queasy. Savages.

"Or a machine gun," Brian said. "Line them up against the wall and *dang-dang-dang-dang-dang-dang!* The whole rotten bunch of them! All the Nazis!"

"Use his guts for garters," Mrs. Mossop repeated.

"String him from a lamppost," said Mavis.

"Put a tin bucket over Hitler's head and bang it till he goes crazy," said Brian.

At this point, Brin had had enough. "Look, can't we change the subject." But Mrs. Mossop interrupted. "Damn that cat, he's licking the butter off the plates!"

"Save washing them," Brian said. Mavis giggled. Mrs. Mossop began to sing, "We're gonna hang out the washing on the Siegfried Line."

"And that's about all," Brin said to Tello and Madi.

"What were you thinking?" Madi asked.

"I was worried. A bit scared, I suppose. All that talk of violence. And yet—"

He thought of the iron thumping, and the smell of the laundry, and Brian and Mavis sighing over their homework, and Blackie the cat yawning and flexing his claws in front of the kitchen stove . . .

"I don't know," Brin said. "It gets quite cozy among the 'savages'. . . ."

The next evening Brin was back in the scenario.

At nine, Brian yawned and Mavis said, "I'm tired too. I haven't finished my math, though. . . . Oh, the heck with it; I'll finish it over breakfast. You going to bed Brian?"

"S'pose so."

The scenario never changed: at nine o'clock Brian and Mavis were programed to become tired. Just after nine they left the room with Mrs. Mossop's words following them: "Good night and sweet repose, half the bed and all the clothes." She put the irons away, did noisy things to the kitchen stove, sighed, laid a tablecloth over the ironing, got her coat and rusty black hat—which had to be pinned to her hair—and said, "No rest for the wicked. Well, I suppose I must love you and leave you, Master Brin. . . ."

"Good night, Mrs. Mossop!"

"Good night, Master Brin. And don't do nothing I wouldn't do."

She would glance at Blackie suspiciously and deliver her last words. "Don't you forget to put Hitler out, Master Brin!"

"I won't forget, Mrs. Mossop."

"Ta-ta, then,"

"Ta-ta."

Mavis and Brian were gone; Mrs. Mossop was gone—put back in their boxes behind the dresser, gone to limbo until the next day when the players would return to their little stage.

There was nowhere else for them to go, of course. No bathroom and bedrooms upstairs, no father and mother. The rest of the house and its people did not exist except in their minds.

Only Blackie the cat "existed" for twenty-four hours a day. Like Brin, he lived inside and outside the scenario.

Brin sighed and yawned and scratched his left armpit. Behind him, the big kitchen dresser swung silently on its hidden hinges. Madi was there. "Anything to discuss?"

"No. Nothing."

"You're bored, aren't you?"

"Yes."

"And worried about something. Worried about what?"

"Well, they're intelligent. They're living, breathing, intelligent human beings. How much longer do you expect them to act out the same old scene in the same old place?"

"As long as we want them to," Madi replied.

"Suppose they don't want to? Suppose they get tired of it?"

"They're programed," Madi reminded him. "They have to follow the scenario. They can't change."

She was wrong.

"I'm sick of this," Brian said, kicking his book bag and thumping his elbows down on the kitchen table.

"Stop it! You're shaking the table!" Mavis was doing her homework.

"Who cares?" Brian said. "I'm sick of homework, too. And sick of you. Sick of everything."

Mrs. Mossop sang, " 'I Lift Up My Finger and I Say, Tweet, Tweet, Now, Now, Hush, Hush, Come, Come!' "

"And I'm sick of your singing, too," Brian told her. His face turned red.

Mavis looked up from her work. "Don't you speak to Mrs. Mossop like that!"

"I jolly well will!"

"You jolly well say you're sorry!"

"I jolly well won't. So there."

Brin looked at Mrs. Mossop. She held a hot iron in her big red hand. Brin cringed. The stout arm lifted, the heavy hand and iron lifted—

Thump went the iron, on the ironing board. Brin let out his breath and felt his heart stop pounding. The weathered face showed no emotion. The iron went back and forth smoothing a napkin.

"She gets the words of the song wrong," Brian said feebly, after a long pause. "It isn't 'Tweet, Tweet, Now, Now, Hush—' "

"What is it then, big mouth?" said Mavis. She looked at her brother's troubled face and hissed, "Say you're sorry."

He muttered, "Sorry, Mrs. Mossop, I didn't mean—"

Without looking at him she sang, " 'You Always Hurt the One You Love,' " then said, with an air of surprise, "Hey, where is his lordship? Where's Hitler been and gone? Where's Blackie?"

Brian jumped up. "I'll go and see, Mrs. Mossop. He ought to be here!"

He went into the scullery and banged around, hiding his embarrassment by making a lot of noise. Mavis started to say something to Mrs. Mossop, but she wouldn't listen. She said, "Lord bless you, he meant no harm. Damn this iron, it's colder'n yesterday's leg of lamb."

"I can't find Blackie, Mrs. Mossop!" Brian said.

"Have you looked in the toilet, outside?" Mavis asked him.

"Yes. The larder, the scullery, the toilet—"

"He's in the garden, then, catching things," Mrs. Mossop said. "Hope it's a rabbit, we'll have stew, I don't think." She looked up worriedly, forgetting her ironing, and began to call, "Blackie—Blackie—Blackie, come along, then!" in a high, thin voice.

Brian said, "I'll go and look for him in the garden."

Brin panicked: there was no garden. "You can't do that!" he told Brian sharply.

"Oh, can't I? Who says so? Why not?" Brian demanded.

"I mean," Brin said, "it's dark out there. Pitch black. You can't find a black cat in a dark—"

"I'll get my flashlight," Brian said. "From the bedroom." He stared at Brin. "You've turned a funny color," he said.

"I'll get your flashlight," Brin said—wondering if Madi could produce one.

"No you won't," Brian said, suspiciously. "I'll get it." He stared at Brin. "Have you been playing with my flashlight?"

"No! Of course not. I just said I'd go and get it—"

"So you must know where it is?"

"No, I heard you *say* it was in your bedroom—"

"If you know where I left it, you must have been messing around with it! Wasting the batteries!"

"I *haven't* been wasting the batteries!"

"Oh, so you admit you've been using it?" said Brian triumphantly.

Then Brin felt a sensation he had never felt before: something hard hit his face—something that jarred him, shook him. He saw little colored lights and then felt what he knew to be pain, real pain. The pain came from where he had been hit.

Brian had hit him in the face with his fist.

He shook his head and peered through the pain at Brian. People did not hit people—that was the First Law. The Sleepers did not let you hit people either. He had never been hit, but now someone had hit him. So Brian *was* a savage. . . .

But Brian did not look like a savage. He, too, looked shocked, he looked just what Brin felt: embarrassed. He was backing away from Brin, his mouth trying to say words.

Mavis was hitting Brian, slapping at him and pulling at his hair and shouting, "Pig! You're a spoiled, stupid, bad-tempered *pig!*"

Brian broke away from her and ran to the scullery door. He turned and shouted, "I—I don't care! And I'm going to find Blackie!" He turned to run through the scullery, out of the back door, into the garden that did not exist.

Brin shouted, "Please! Don't! Brian! Come back!"

Then Brian was floundering around in the scullery—he had tripped on the step and fallen. Mavis was crying—and Mrs. Mossop was deliberately looking down at her work and going thump with the iron, not paying attention—

The scream of a bomb grew from nothing, getting louder and louder, a whining shriek that came nearer and nearer, so loud that it drowned the throbbing drone of the German bombers up there—

The bomb exploded, so close that the whole house shook and the glass in the big kitchen windows rattled and you could hear a house crashing and tinkling and thundering down into rubble only just down the road—

The lights flickered, and Blackie rushed out from behind the icebox where he had been sleeping, with his eyes ablaze and his tail like a bottlebrush—

Brian had not gone into the garden that did not exist.

Later, Madi said, "I don't know what you are worried about. The 'bomb' did what we wanted done. It stopped the situation dead."

Brin said, "It could have killed everyone!"

"Don't be ridiculous, Brin. You don't really think for one moment that—"

"You mean, it *wasn't* a bomb?"

"Really, Brin! Of course not. Just a recording."

"But the windows shook, the house shook—"

"It was a very *loud* recording, Brin. Loud sounds are made by moving a great deal of air. The movement of a great deal of air makes windows and houses shake."

He said nothing and felt foolish. Eventually he mumbled, "A sledgehammer to crack a nut."

"What did you say, Brin?"

"Old saying. They use it. 'A sledgehammer to crack a nut' means using something much too big to achieve something small."

"What would *you* have done to stop Brian from going into the garden—to make him change his mind in a split second?" Madi asked.

"I don't know. . . . Did you see Brian hit me?"

"Yes. Quite a violent evening. But then, those were violent times. World War II, remember. The Blitz . . . the bombing raids on London . . ."

"I don't see why you couldn't have done it without bombers and bombs."

"Ah, but those bombs might be useful!" she said. Then she flinched.

Brian saw her. "What do you mean? What do you mean? Useful for what? What do you mean, *'useful'?*"

Smoothly she said, "Useful to make a violent interruption when something goes wrong within the scenario. As it did tonight. Even more useful to find out how our Reborns stand up to danger, fear, pressure."

"You're not telling me everything, Madi!"

"Nor will I, Brin. I will see you tomorrow. Meanwhile, go to bed."

"Listen, Madi!"

"Good night, Brin. Do stop worrying. There's nothing to worry about."

She smiled.

There was no trouble for three more evenings.

They walked of the bomb—"No. 37 down the road, completely flattened! Well, anyhow, the garage is, and all the windows."

They talked about homework—"You're lucky, Brin, not to have homework to do. When is your uncle coming? No, I suppose you wouldn't know. Not with a war on."

They had crumpets, played with Blackie.

One whole evening went by playing Monopoly. The game was so good that Brin wanted to stay to the end and Madi "got" his thought. That night, bedtime was after ten, an hour after Mrs. Mossop had left. Mavis won and did handstands to celebrate until her face was scarlet.

It amused Brin to hear her say, next evening, "Can't we play a game? *Do* something?" She had no memory of the game played the evening before. The game had been wiped off Brian's and Mavis's memory program. Brian said, "There's a Monopoly set somewhere, let's play that." And Mavis replied, "Oh, I can't stand that game, it's dull, and goes on and on. . . . Let's play ludo."

On the fourth day, Brian said, "I wish I were older."

"Why?" Mavis asked.

"Well, missing the war and everything. If I were only a few years older, I'd be *in* it. Flying a Spitfire. . . ."

"You flying a *Spitfire!* Ha *ha!"*

Brian was too gloomy to reply. He poked at his geography book with the nib of his fountain pen, leaving little blue-black insect marks on the cover. "Your uncle is in the RAF, isn't he?" he asked Brin.

"Yes," Brin said.

"Well, when's he coming over?"

"I've told you, I don't know."

"Does he fly?"

"Yes, but he's a scientific expert."

"Wish I were an expert. . . ." Brian said. The pen spattered a little fleck of ink on Mavis's leg. She said, "Oh, really, must you!" Then, peevish, she said, "I can't imagine *anything* a stupid inky schoolboy would be wanted for in this or any other war!"

"There's Civil Defense." Brian said. "The air-raid wardens have to have runners, don't they? Boys on bikes or something, to take messages, I could do that."

"No you couldn't," Mavis said. "You're too young. They wouldn't accept you. And anyhow, both your tires are flat, you don't take care of that bike at all."

"It's just that I'm sick of hanging around," he said. "Sick of this kitchen, and doing homework and cleaning shoes for tomorrow. . . ."

"You haven't cleaned the shoes tonight, so I don't see how you can be fed up," Mavis said. "Hadn't you better clean them now, and get it over with?"

"Oh, shut *up.*"

"Shut up yourself! And if," she continued, "you're going to act like a camel with the hump, why don't you go somewhere else to do it? You've got a room of your own, you know!"

Brin became alert. The room was a false memory. It existed only in Brian's memory.

Brian began to clean his sister's shoes as well as his own. Mavis put the dishes away and set a tray for breakfast. That was the arrangement. Tonight, Brian worked slowly, dully and badly.

Mrs. Mossop said, "Well, I can tell you're a good soldier, Master Brian!"

"What do you mean, good soldier?" he grumbled.

"Because you never look behind you!" she said, and smiled to herself.

"What do you mean, never look—"

Mavis giggled. "Don't you get it?" she said. "Do you

honestly mean you don't *get* it? You're not doing the *heels* properly, stupid! You're not looking *behind* you."

Before Brin could even flash a thought at Madi, Brian had thrown the shoes and polish and brushes in the corner and was walking toward the kitchen door. Fortunately he turned before Brin had to prevent him from leaving. "If you think I'm staying here to listen to your stupid jokes you've got another think coming! Because I'm not!" ("Come on, Madi, come on!" Brin prayed.) "I'm sick of it here!" Brian raged. "Sick of everything!"

The air-raid warning sounded just in time.

As the sirens wailed, Brian paused, his hand still on the doorknob.

Mavis said, "Brian, come back, don't be so silly—" but he turned the knob.

Mrs. Mossop looked at Brian through her gold-rimmed glasses, thumped down the iron and said, "Old Nasty's up there, and we're down here and we need a man about the house! Now then, Master Brian!"

Brian came back and Brin breathed easily.

"It's not going to last," Brin told Madi. "It can't go on much longer. Someone's going to break out of the scenario. Most probably Brian, but Mavis might do it too. You can't tell with her."

"They'll do what they're told," Madi said.

"No they won't. They're not like us. They don't obey, instinctively. Well, not instinctively," he corrected himself, "but they don't have Sleepers. . . ."

"They'll obey." Her voice was flatly certain.

"They won't, Madi. They won't."

He left Madi and went off on his own. He was fed up. Had he caught his mood from Brian and Mavis? Very probably. He was sick of the scenario, sick of the kitchen and scullery and larder and the outside toilet—as sick of it as they were.

Yet Mavis and Brian could not remember it all. Each evening was a new evening to them. To Brin it was the same dreary old play, to be enacted yet again. To them games of Monopoly or ludo were new each time. To Brin they were a bore.

"I'm more sorry for me than I am for them," he thought gloomily. And Madi and Tello were no help. They seemed uninterested yet completely sure of themselves. As if Brin were of no importance.

He decided he needed exercise. He headed for the Sports Center. The brilliant lights of the community's gleaming buildings, all metal and glass and plastic, reflected on the moving walkways. Today was a rain day, Brin remembered. He stepped on the moving walkway and let it take him to the center, watching the play of reflected lights shift beneath his feet as the moving surfaces contrasted with the unmoving surroundings. Pretty.

But then his mind went back to Brian and Mavis. He thought about their stubbornness, quarrelsomeness and toughness. He saw in his mind the strong, unchangeable figure of Mrs. Mossop, forever bent over her ironing, forever singing snatches of popular songs. "Strangers!" he said out loud. "Foreigners! Aliens!" And yet he liked them. He had to admit that he liked them. Did he like them more than the people of his own time, so obedient and peaceful and clever? More than himself?

He was so deep in thought that he went past the center. He hopped tracks, angry with himself, and got on the moving walkway going the opposite way. Sixty-five stories high, a third of a mile wide, the center blazed with colored lights. Solid pictures, holographs, tumbled and whirled. Three-dimensional acrobats hurtled past the lit windows, dancing girls beckoned, voices and music cooed or bellowed with every few feet the walkway traveled. Brin thought, "That looks good: *The Venus Explosion*. Shall I see that?" But he was in the wrong mood for it. The holographs showed vast explosions—molten rocks hurtled at Brin's face, one seemed to pass through his body, the noise was deafening—no, not that. Wrong mood.

The traveling walkway took him to Entrance G. G for Gymnastics. "Yes," Brin said to himself, and got off. Gymnastics might not have too many people or too much noise.

The uniformed girl at the reception desk smiled at him. "What sport?" Brin thought about it for a minute or two and said, "Is the Nograv full tonight?" She touched a switch: only two or three people could be seen on the screen. "You'll have it almost to yourself," she said, still smiling brightly.

She had beautiful legs, bare and slender. They reminded Brin of Mavis's legs, in the wrinkled gray stockings, and Brian's scarred and inky knees.

The smiling girl said, "Nograv okay for you, then?"

"Yes. Fine."

"Check your record?"

Automatically he held out his left wrist to show her his ID band—the bracelet that told the state and its officials everything they needed to know about him. The information was contained in a bright dot, like the eye of a small bird, welded to the band. The ID band fitted so smoothly and snugly that you forgot you wore it. But you wore it all the time. That was the law.

"Hey!" said the girl. She was not smiling anymore. She was staring at Brin. "Check your record, I said. Well?"

"What? Oh!" Brin felt his face turn red. He fumbled in the pockets of his track suit. Where had he put his ID band? He'd removed it when he changed for his evening in the scenario with Mavis and Brian, changed back to his usual clothes afterward and forgotten to put it back on.

"Here it is," he said, taking it from his pocket.

"Put it on your *wrist*. Show it to me on your *wrist*," the girl said.

He did as he was told. She jerked her head at the Chek and he put his left hand flat on the Chek panel. There was the usual little click as the Chek accepted him and his ID band, but the girl said, "That's a *fault*, you know. Not wearing your band. You do know that's a fault?"

"Yes. But—"

"You *do* know I'm supposed to report faults?"

"Yes. Look, it won't happen again, it was just—"

"How many faults make a demerit?" she insisted.

"Three. Look, I haven't got any *other* faults, the Chek would have told you if I had other faults—"

"You kids," the girl said. "Just because you're kids, you think you can get away with anything."

"So you won't report me?"

"What's the use," she said, wearily and scornfully. "You're a kid, you're the little darling of the universe. No, I won't report you. But next time you wear your ID band. You wear it *all the time*, okay?"

"Okay." He touched his heart and brain in the Sign of Politeness.

She turned her back on him even while she repeated the sign. He picked up his gear and walked to the Nograv, in a gloomier mood than ever.

The Nograv always made him feel better. And this evening there were only two other people in it, both of them quite old, and content to flip about quietly without shouting or showing off.

Brin thrust off from the wall and let himself float the whole sixty meters across to the other wall, fast and smooth and almost straight—just a slight curl of the spine to bring his knees up as the opposite wall rushed to meet him. *Boompf!* The soft shock of his bare feet against the soft, springy wall, then bounce back across the huge padded Nograv cell, flying so easily, so smoothly . . . because he was weightless. Free from the pull of the earth's gravity, any gravity. Freer than a bird.

Boompf. Boompf.

He let himself bounce from wall to wall, feeling his muscles stretch, feeling his almost naked body released from its own weights and tensions. Beneath him, the two other people had joined hands, they were going to try a blast-off. Their hands and feet met, their arm and leg muscles tensed as they strained against each other, then—ah!—they exploded apart, arching backward, spinning as they flew outward, locking their arms around their knees to speed the spin . . . *boompf!*

The man timed it wrong, he hit the wall with his back, but the woman got it exactly right—feet against the wall, a quick straightening of the legs, and she was rocketing from the wall with the lights crisscrossing her flying body, her hair streaming out behind her. She did a flip against the opposite wall to kill her speed. Brin heard her laugh at the man, who was spinning himself in a backward arc waiting for her to join him and try again. He was laughing apologetically.

Brin smiled and flew gently to the padded bars, springy and soft in his hands. He began to loop, faster and faster, hanging on until the speed was just right—then let go. The other bars rushed toward him. A catch-hold—*now*—and away again, the third bar was in his hands, his spin was reversed, still faster, and—*now*—his feet touched another bar but he missed the hook-on. . . .

He tried again, forgetting Mavis and Brian and Mrs.

Mossop and Madi and Reborns; forgetting everything but his own body and the soft shock of the walls and getting the loops and hook-ons and catch-holds and reverses exactly right.

Later, the adults who had been with him in the Nograv offered him a snack in the diner. They turned out to be pleasant, though a little too "nice" and full of admiring smiles. But then, of course, as Brin knew, adults felt they had to be like that with young people: important people.

Next day was another bad day. The Seniors called him before them.

Senior Tello sat beside him this time, facing the big curved table. So did Madi. "Senior Tello, you don't mind sitting with the boy?" said the Senior Elect. He had pretended to be peevish at the very first meeting; this time his peevishness seemed real.

"No, we're both observers—reporters—in this matter," Tello said, smiling to himself. "And I'm honored," he continued, "to sit beside such an important person as our young friend Brin. . . ."

Brin could not tell if Tello was laughing at him. The faces of the Seniors told him nothing.

"Let's get on with it," said the Senior Elect.

"Well, I've been with the Reborns for twenty-three evenings now," Brin began. But the Senior Elect interrupted him. "Yes, well, we'll come to you in a minute. Senior Tello?"

Tello stood up. As he talked, he walked back and forth,

his white robe swirling. His voice was not only deep and beautiful, but humorous—almost offhand. Brin found himself listening to the voice rather than the words. They hardly mattered. Tello was reporting things that Brin already knew.

But he paid close attention when Tello explained how he and Madi monitored the scenario. "We are behind the big closet called the kitchen dresser," Tello explained. "I am there sometimes. Madi is always there."

"What are you doing when you are not there?" said the Senior Elect.

"I review the telerecordings and correct the scenario, making sure that unforeseen circumstances do not develop into dangerous situations," Tello said.

"For instance?"

"The chief danger is that the Reborns will try to escape from the scenario."

"You mean, just walk out of it?"

"Yes. If one of them did that, there would be a complication of *place*. There is nothing beyond the scenario except a brief space of nothingness—a limbo—leading to the real world, our world. The scenario is in a black bubble, so to speak. The Reborns must never try to penetrate it."

"What would happen if they did?" asked the Chinese Senior.

"The experiment would be wasted," said Tello. They would no longer be able to believe in their roles. They would be useless to us, which would be tragic."

"Tragic?" said the Senior Elect. "Wasteful, perhaps.

Hardly tragic. We could always recondition them—give them new memory patterns."

"I think not," Tello said. "We are not trying to discover what we can *make* them do. We are trying to discover what they want to do. How they *want* to behave."

The horse-faced Senior said, "I see what Tello means. Stress, anger, revolt, uneasiness, irritability—we must let the Reborns express these emotions as freely as possible, without conditioning. We must see them as they really are. Is that right, Tello?"

"Exactly right. We must condition them to the minimum degree necessary and stimulate them to the maximum degree. When we've pushed them to the limit, we will know their true natures. Then we can decide how useful they can be to us later as parents and founders of new generations—"

"Stop it," shouted Brin. "You go on about anger, revolt and irritability, but that's not all Mavis and Brian show. Or Mrs. Mossop. They behave less cruelly than you do!"

"Don't be impertinent," said the Senior Elect.

Brin stormed on. "They're not just savages and idiots, leftovers from another age! They're real people! And I don't like the way you talk about them," he ended feebly. He felt foolish. He didn't know why he had defended the Reborns. Why should they matter to him?

The Senior Elect raised his eyebrows and looked at Madi. "Well, Madi?"

"I'll confine myself to facts," she said carefully. "Brian and Mavis are larger and physically stronger than most children of our time, their heads and cranial capacities are smaller—"

"You mean, their brains are small? They are less intelligent?" asked the Chinese Senior.

"Their brains are smaller, but their intelligence seems —different. Not necessarily smaller."

"Because they don't have Sleepers? They're merely conditioned?"

"Because they are ruled by their *emotions,* just as we are ruled by our Sleepers. For hundreds of years our civilization has been based on achieving peace—peace between nations and peoples, peace between person and person. But for hundreds of thousands of years, the old people and their civilization relied on war—conflict between nations and people, conflicts between person and person. Even the games children played in those days were competitive. And as you know, we have placed our Reborns in a period of world war."

Brin interrupted again. "They should have been given peaceful, happy lives."

"Peace," the horse-faced Senior explained, "is too slow for our purpose. We must force the pace. The Reborns must act out a forceful, even dangerous, play. Things must happen fast."

The Seniors went on talking. Brin did not listen. He had other things to puzzle and worry him.

One of the things that puzzled and worried him most was his left armpit.

Brin's left armpit itched.

It had itched for a long time. Long before the Reborns and the scenario.

The itch had become worse after his Nograv session. Brin thought it must be caused by the exercise. He had stood in front of the mirror in the changing rooms, lifted his arm and examined his armpit. He saw little red dots, pinpricks.

He was not surprised to see the dots. Everyone had them. But on other people, they were almost invisible. Brin knew they were identification marks in an isotope code. If you were involved in an accident that destroyed your ID band, there were still the permanent codes pricked into your left armpit.

Some of the marks meant "extras." On the rare occasion when a baby was born, the proud parents were told, "There! A real baby! Your baby! Now, do you wish to apply for extras? Any special preferences and needs?"

The parents might reply, "Well, ours is a very musical family. . . ."

"Then let's reinforce the baby's musical aptitude. Anything else?"

"I've never been very good with my hands. Always a bit clumsy."

"Digital dexterity, then. We'll give your baby an extra for that."

There would be a few routine jokes made about fairy godmothers—the baby would be given implants, or a modified Sleeper, or anything else needed—and the isotopic pinpricks would record the fact, just as they recorded all other essential facts about you.

That day in the Nograv, the man Brin met had said, "I'm still not much good, but I'm getting better each session. I applied for an extra in physical dexterity. A late extra; they let me take my extra only eight months ago. Nice of them. And it's working! Mind you," he added, "the pinprick still itches a bit. But they warned me of that."

Brin had never asked for or been given any late extras. Yet his left armpit itched. And the pinpricks were raw and red, as if they were recent.

Since meeting the man in the Nograv, Brin's mind, like his left armpit, had never stopped itching. There was something wrong.

Mavis hobbled into the kitchen at the beginning of the next act of the scenario, with blood already thick and blackened on her knee and with red blood still running down the stocking on her leg.

Brin felt sick. He had never seen flowing blood—not even his own. He had never seen a wound that was not cured, instantly, by a medipac—you slapped the pack on, the wound healed. He and his friends seldom, if ever, injured themselves. The discipline of the Sleepers made them avoid danger. If the Sleepers failed, there were medipacs. If the medipacs failed, there were DomDocs—the domestic doctor units fitted in every public and private place. If the DomDoc could not take care of it, only the ambulance crew ever saw the injury.

Mavis was not really crying, she was whimpering. Her nostrils were white and she trembled. Brin started to go to her but he felt faint. It was Brian who supported her and led her to a chair; Brian who got warm water and disinfectant, and cut away the stocking and cleaned the wound.

All Brin could do was to look away from the bleeding flesh, and curse Madi and Tello and anyone else involved in inventing such a cruel program for Mavis. Someone, Brin realized, must actually have hit Mavis—hurt her while she slept.

Now, with her wound cleaned and wrapped in a handkerchief, Mavis was really crying. Brian, awkward yet determined, bent over her, his head touching hers and his red hand patting her shoulder. "It's all right, old girl," he kept saying. "It's all right, old girl. . . ." Saying the strange words—"old girl"—cost Brian an effort, Brin could see. An effort of tenderness. He had never call her "old girl" before, only "Mave" or "M."

When Mavis stopped crying and let her head rest against Brian, Brin saw that Brian's eyes were filled with tears. Brian tried to pretend they were not there by shaking his head or furtively brushing his sleeve over his eyes, but a tear fell on the crown of Mavis's head. She must have felt its wet coldness as it trickled through her hair, for she looked up and said, "You old sissy!" and began to laugh.

"Don't know what you mean," Brian said, hoarsely.

"You're an old sissy!" she said, laughing and blowing her nose.

"Sissy yourself," Brian said. "Sobbing like that. . . . How's the knee?"

"Much better, thank you very much," said Mavis, suddenly solemnly polite, as if she were a little girl politely saying good-bye to her host at a party. "Stupid bike," she said. "Stupid rotten front brake. . . ."

She got up and, deliberately and carefully, put her arms around her brother's neck and kissed him. He looked almost frightened, yet he kissed her cheek hastily. "I'll make tea," he mumbled, and he went to the scullery and filled the kettle.

When Mrs. Mossop arrived, it was as if a party were going on. Brian and Mavis were stabbing the sausages they were to have for supper with forks, dangling them in front of the cat, pretending they were the enemy—"This one's Hitler, this one's Mussolini!"—stab, stab. Brian tried to balance a sausage on his nose.

Mrs. Mossop said, "Well, I must say! Very cheerful we are tonight, aren't we!" She switched on her light and began ironing, listening and watching as Mavis acted out falling off her bicycle and cutting her knee open. She did it so well that even Brin roared with laughter.

"And what did you make of them this evening?" asked Madi.

"You saw it all yourself," said Brin. He did not want to talk about it. He felt a private warmth for Mavis and Brian that he did not want to share or discuss, particularly with Madi. He felt she could not understand.

"An extraordinary performance!" she said coolly. "Extraordinary!" said Brin, and left it at that.

Later, though, he attacked her. "Did you have to hurt Mavis that much? Was that what the Seniors meant by 'making things less boring'?"

Madi shrugged.

"Did you see the wound?"

"Not close up." Madi sniffed.

"Well, I did. You think Mavis and Brian are savage, crude, brutal. . . . But you don't seem to mind doing savage and crude things to them—"

"You're not making much sense, and I've got to go," Madi said. She went away, leaving Brin to his thoughts.

He thought about the rest of that evening in the scenario. When the sausages had been cooked and eaten, and Mrs. Mossop had gone and the party had quieted down, Brian had brought up the old subject again. "Your uncle," he said. "I wish he'd come. I want to *see* him. . . ."

"*I* want to see him too," Mavis said. "I want something to happen! I want *him* to happen. When is he coming?"

"I don't know," Brin said. "It could be anytime." Then, seeing their faces fall, he added, "Soon, I suppose. Quite soon."

"Let's have another look at his picture," Mavis said.

Brin gave her the photograph and she studied it. "His hair's sort of brown, isn't it?"

"Yes. Darkish brown."

"He's got a little mole on his face. Or is it the photograph?"

"No, it's like that. A mole. Very small."

"He's got nice hands. Did he always have a moustache?"

"As long as I can remember," Brin lied.

"Is he under or over six feet tall? Does he smoke?"

"Just over six foot, I think. I'm not sure if he smokes. He used to, but not much."

Brian took the photograph and studied it carefully. "If he's got medals for flying, why doesn't he fly?"

"I told you, he's not a flying type anymore. He's a scientist."

"But I bet he flies sometimes."

"Yes, I suppose so."

"If he's a test pilot, he must have had a chance to fly all sorts of planes. . . . I bet he's flown more airplanes than any ordinary pilot!"

Brin let his vanity carry him away. "Well," he said, pretending to make an effort, "I know he's flown Spitfires and Hurricanes, because he started out as a fighter pilot—"

"Fighter pilot!" Brian said. "In Hurricanes and Spits! Lucky him!"

"And I think he did a conversion course for bombers," Brin said. "Wellingtons, I suppose. And Beauforts. I know he's flown Beauforts. Fighter-bombers. And some of the newer types. But of course, he doesn't tell *me* much. He can't. Official secrets."

"Was he ever shot down?"

Brin screwed up his eyes to look wise and, proud of his knowledge of the language of the period, said, "Not shot

down. But he was shot *up,* over the English Channel. In a
Beaufort. They were strafing enemy shipping and got
hit."

"Was he wounded?" Mavis said breathlessly.

"No. But his gunner was. And the radio op." Brin
combed his memory for the crew of a Beaufort. Did it
carry a radio operator? Probably. "The radio op got it the
worst," he said, shaking his head. "But my uncle got them
back to base okay. Had to land with the undercarriage up.
Belly landing."

"Gosh!" Mavis said. Then, "I do wish he'd come. I do
wish we could see him, here. I want to meet somebody
real. . . ."

"Somebody really *doing* something," Brian murmured.
"Somebody *real.* . . ."

Brin tried to change the subject. He felt guilty and
ashamed.

"Why did you need Mrs. Mossop?" Brin asked Madi and
Tello. "Why was she made a Reborn?"

"Why do you need walls in the Nograv?" Tello replied,
smiling.

"To bounce off," Brin said sourly.

"Quite right. Mrs. Mossop provides Brian and Mavis
with something to bounce off. Children were used to the
constant presence of adults in those days. They lived with
their parents and other grown-ups. Not like today."

"But Mrs. Mossop must have taken a lot of making.
And she's old. It seems a waste. You don't want old peo-

ple, you want young people. People of my age—old enough to understand what you teach them, young enough to be conditioned by the teaching. Isn't that right?"

"Absolutely right. But Mrs. Mossop was . . . found, and she fitted in with the period and pattern. So we made her as a companion for Mavis and Brian."

"What do you mean, she was found?" Brin asked. "What was found?"

"Enough to work with," Tello said, not smiling.

"You mean, her dead body?"

"Parts of it."

"And her clothing?"

"Parts of it."

"A rag, a bone and a hank of hair," Brin said.

"What was that?"

"Nothing. Just a quotation. A writer called Kipling made up those words about a woman."

"Oh, I see," Tello said. He yawned. "So there you are then, Brin. The twentieth century left a rag, a bone and a hank of hair, and we created Mrs. Mossop from them." He looked at Brin inquiringly as if asking, "Any more questions?"

"Where did you find her?" Brin asked.

"Oh, in West London. She must have died in a bombing raid in the Hitler war. Her components were completely buried."

"Her components?" Brin did not like the word.

"The rags and bones and hanks of hair," Tello said,

looking directly at Brin. Brin could think of nothing to say. He did not like the pictures forming in his mind. Eventually he said, "She's a nice old lady."

"A *useful* old lady," Tello said, smiling again. He got up and stretched. He looked very tall and powerful, Brin thought—just as Madi, quietly sitting and making notes, looked clean, young, firm, decisive and elegant.

Not at all like Mrs. Mossop.

When Mrs. Mossop arrived the next evening, she seemed the same as ever and yet completely different. She seemed smaller.

Brian and Mavis noticed the change straight away. Brin did not. There was silence as Mrs. Mossop got out her ironing board, and heated the irons. It was the awkwardness of the silence that made Brin realize that something unusual had happened to Mrs. Mossop.

But nothing was said. Brian and Mavis did their homework. When her iron was hot and ready, she went *thump . . . thump* just as usual. But she did not sing.

And suddenly there was the smell of scorched linen. Mrs. Mossop was thumping the same piece of ironing again and again, not looking at it, staring straight ahead of herself, not seeing the brown scorch marks she was making.

Mavis ran to her and touched her arm and said, "Mrs. Mossop . . ." But the old lady didn't seem to hear her. The iron went *thump* on the scorch. There was a little smoke.

Mrs. Mossop saw the smoke and said, "Damn the

devil!" Then she put the iron on its end so that it could do no more damage, threw her apron over her head, sat down in a chair and began to say, "Damn him! Damn and blast him!" Her shoulders shook and her thin gold wedding ring glinted under the electric light against her strong, wrinkled fingers.

"It's the woman next door," she said a little later. "Mrs. Hills. She's gone, and the house with her. It's all gone, all gone. And her with a son in the Merchant Navy. . . ."

Brin noticed that Mavis and Brian said nothing. They moved about slowly, not looking at the old lady, not answering anything she said. They got cups and saucers, filled the kettle, warmed the pot and made tea. All this time, Mrs. Mossop talked, dabbing at her eyes behind her gold-rimmed glasses, telling them of the raid last night: of the land mine, and the houses flattened, and the fire engines and ambulances and the Civil Defense and Mrs. Hills being dragged out—"but it was no use, you could see at a glance, she was gone. We was neighbors twenty-three years, that's a long time. . . ."

They gave her tea. She drank a little of it and said, "I *do* like a cup of tea. . . ."

They talked to her, soothingly. She answered normally. Once she broke into a swearing tirade about Hitler, using words that even Brin knew to be forbidden. But then she said, "Oh dear, oh dear, I beg your pardon, you mustn't mind me. I'm not myself and that's a fact. . . ."

Brin thought, "No, you're not. You're an old woman now, an old, old woman."

Using the ugliest of the words he had learned from Mrs. Mossop, he cursed everyone involved with the Reborn program. They had made Mrs. Mossop weak and old and tearful just as an "experiment." It was cruel. It was wrong.

Mrs. Mossop left early. There was silence when she was gone. Brin broke the silence by saying, "It's rotten! Poor Mrs. Mossop! What's she done to deserve—"

Brian said, "No good talking about it. Change the subject."

Brin turned to Mavis, shocked by Brian's apparent coldness, but she, too, said, "Talk about something else."

"*What* else?" Brin demanded.

"I don't know. Anything. Oh, I know—tell us more about your Uncle Rick!"

Brin tried to get out of it, but couldn't. And for the next hour he made up stories about his uncle, stories so exciting that Mavis's eyes sparkled and Brian said, "Gosh! Go on! What happened next?"

Brin invented thrill upon thrill. After all, it was better than thinking about Mrs. Mossop. . . .

To the Elders, however, Brin spoke what was in his mind when he appeared before them.

By now he felt he knew them. Tello was almost his friend. The horse-faced Senior turned out to be a surprisingly warm, pleasant woman. The Chinese-looking Senior was a discreet, private person whose smile, Brin now knew, meant very little—it was as if she put her smile on in the morning with her clothes and wore it all day. But she listened carefully when Brin spoke, then smiled and nodded agreement.

The other Seniors, too, were now familiar figures in Brin's mind. Not friends; neutrals. Standing (or more likely sitting) before the white-gowned figures of the Seniors had never frightened Brin. He was too conscious of the superiority of his youth to feel fear. He felt only tension: a tightening of his mental muscles. He was always aware that he had to keep his mind alert and fast-moving, his words clear and vivid, his face and manner decisive.

Today he felt nothing of this familiar tension. He felt only a deep and determined anger that he intended to express.

The Seniors made the Sign of Politeness. Brin barely bothered to sketch his reply. Before his hands had stopped moving, he was speaking. "About Mrs. Mossop," he said. His voice was cold and clear. "What you did to her was savage, stupid and brutal." He folded his arms across his chest and sat back in his chair, watching the faces of the Seniors.

Their reactions were not at all what he expected

The Chinese Senior smiled and nodded. The horse-faced Senior turned her head very slightly to one side and looked back levelly into Brin's eyes with an expression of friendly interest. The Senior Elect continued to write with his old-fashioned pen on a tablet of paper, without even looking up. Tello took no notice at all of Brin. Brin was surprised and hurt.

Only Madi seemed aware of the importance of what Brin had said—of the rude violence of his words and the sincerity behind them. She had been standing beside him. Now he felt her hip against his shoulder and heard a whispered, warning murmur, "Brin! You shouldn't—"

At last the Senior Elect looked up and said, "What? What was that, Brin? I don't think I heard. . . . His faded yet piercing eyes were locked on Brin's, expecting and demanding that the words be repeated.

Brin steeled himself and said again, "What you did to Mrs. Mossop was savage, stupid and brutal."

This time the words seemed to echo in the big room.

"Savage," said the Senior Elect, tonelessly. "Ah yes. Savage . . . stupid . . . brutal." He wrote the words down. The Chinese Senior smiled. Tello brooded. The horse-faced Senior began rubbing her long nose with a long finger. To Brin the silence was like a long, cold corridor.

"Is that all you want to say?" asked the Senior Elect.

Brin did not want to reply. He did not trust his voice to stay steady. He gulped and opened his mouth—

The Senior Elect held up a thin hand to prevent him from speaking. "You don't say 'unnecessary,'" he said, mildly. " 'Unnecessary' isn't one of your words. So I suppose you understand that our treatment of Mrs. Mossop was *necessary*. Now, had you said the word 'unnecessary,' Brin, I would have been obliged to reply by saying to you—" He broke off and turned to the other Seniors. "What would I have said to him, do you think?"

The Chinese Senior smiled brightly at Brin and in her

high, clipped voice suggested, " 'Don't be a silly boy!'
Something like that, perhaps?" The Senior Elect nodded
approvingly.

" 'Don't be an impertinent child,' " suggested the
horse-faced Senior.

" 'Shut your stupid mouth!' " said another Senior.

Brin's mouth opened and closed soundlessly. The big
room seemed to spin around him. They were being rude!
Deliberately rude! To him! To Brin! And Tello said nothing. He did not even look up.

"No," said the Senior Elect, "none of you conveys quite
my meaning. Now let me see, let me see. . . . Ah, I have it.
A long time ago, Brin, there was a little poem that fond
parents spoke to their children. I will recite that poem to
you and you will memorize it. This is the poem:

> *Speak when you're spoken to,*
> *Do as you're bid,*
> *Close the door after you,*
> *There's a good kid.*

Have you memorized it, Brin?"

The eyes of the Seniors regarded him with mild interest
as Brin struggled to reply. "Yes," he said at last.

"Then let us hear it!" said the Senior Elect. "Recite it
for us, Brin!"

"Speak when you're spoken to," Brin said, chokingly.

"It would be better if you stood up," said the Senior
Elect. "Stand up, Brin, and continue."

"Do as you're bid," Brin said. His knees trembled and

shame and anger gagged him. *"Close the door after you,"* he continued.

The Senior Elect finished the poem for him. *"There's a good kid,"* he said, soothingly and poisonously. "Take him out, Madi. And let him wait somewhere out of people's way until Tello is ready to give him his next instructions." He gave the Sign of Politeness. Brin, hands shaking, let Madi lead him from the room.

At the door, the mild voice of the Senior Elect called, "And close the door after you, Brin, remember? There's a good kid!"

Madi had to lead Brin away from the room. He could not see through his tears of shame and fury. The pity in her voice when she said, "Wait there, Brin," made his pain all the worse.

When she was gone, he rubbed his eyes, and strode to the door of the bleak little waiting room to which Madi had taken him. He twisted the handle of the door. A square panel above the door lit up and showed the word NO; a recorded voice said, "You are not free to leave. Please take a seat. You are not free to leave."

He twisted the handle again, using all his strength. Something gave. The door opened.

"You are not free to leave," the voice bleated. But he left the voice and the building behind him and walked blindly on, faster and faster, into the city.

You were allowed to walk in the city. Few people did: the moving walkways walked for you. But you could walk if you did not mind the curious stares and the possibility of being stopped by the police and asked to identify and explain yourself.

Brin walked, barely knowing he was walking. He walked without seeing the great silver towers, the wide green parks with each tree named and labeled, each bird and animal identified on the TV displays. He automatically wove his way through the silent electric bicycles that glittered like insect swarms in certain streets and special areas.

Above him the clean, glassy building soared fifty stories high, seeming almost to touch the transparent curve of the Ecodome that packaged the city and made its atmosphere. Cars mewed and whined, slowly bumbling along the roads, blindly following the get-you-there tracks under the road surface. Sometimes a line of cars was stopped, each car nudging squishily at the one in front; only then did the "drivers" and passengers look up from their TV screens in the car. Sometimes a "driver" would crossly prod the tabs and buttons in front of him to make the car go forward again, but it made no difference.

Under Brin's feet the city hummed, growled and vibrated. The real business of the city went on below-ground—the sewers and trains, power plants and factories, nature reserves and laboratories, computer complexes and service depots, protein banks and weather-maker plants. . . .

Brin paused, by habit, at one of the city's eight Great Parks. This was the second biggest—almost an acre.

Trees, shrubs, waterfowl on the little lake and people everywhere. . . .

A big colored moth almost flew into Brin's face. Immediately the nearest TV screen showed a still picture of the moth and named it, in English and Latin.

"As if I cared," Brin said.

His left armpit itched abominably. Obviously because he was hot—hot with rage and resentment. He scratched his armpit furtively, hoping no one would see; then, from habit, made the Sign of Politeness to the world in general.

Hot with anger, raging hot . . . and also cold. Cold with fear in the very center of his body. He had misunderstood everything. Particularly the Seniors. He had misunderstood their power, their arrogance, their authority, their certainty, their cruelty.

And he had failed to understand himself. He had thought of himself as a little king, a power in the land, someone automatically entitled to respect and agreement.

He had thought that when he pointed out to the Seniors the errors of their ways—their cold cruelty to a poor, simple old woman—they would be uneasy and ashamed and anxious to oblige him by making things right.

The Seniors had treated him just as they had treated Mrs. Mossop: with a chilling, humiliating show of power. "Don't be a silly boy." "Speak when you're spoken to, do as you're bid."

"I'll show you," Brian snarled. But show them what? He was just a small cog in this big, glittering wheel of a civilization.

His armpit itched so furiously that he sat down, folded his arms and secretly, privately, gave himself the pleasure of a good long scratch. There! Just there! Better! Was anyone watching him? No, once more, just there! Much better. But when he stopped, the itching started again.

He nearly jumped out of his skin when a voice behind him said, "Who are you?" A huge, inhuman figure towered over him, looking at him through masked beetle eyes. A uniform of Adamant: the nozzle of the suit's Viper pointing at him. Policeman. Special Force.

"Check your record," said the policeman, giving the Sign of Politeness. Returning the sign, Brin felt better. The policeman's inhuman voice said a few words, but the words were spoken with the old, familiar tone of respect.

Without bothering to stand up, Brin showed the policeman his ID band. An agreeable grunt came from the mouthpiece of the Adamant suit—"Mmmm. Fine. Everything all right?"

"Fine," said Brin. "Just fine."

"Just a routine check," said the policeman. "Just making sure you're all right."

"I'm all right. Fine. Thank you."

"Have a good day, then. Rain tomorrow, remember! Enjoy the sun today."

"Right."

The policeman gave the Sign of Politeness. Brin returned it. The policeman went away, walking like a broad machine, the man's muscles multiplied by those built into the Adamant suit. Brin watched him go, the sun glinting on the silver-white fabric and the white dome of helmet. Polite policeman. Quite right to be polite.

Brin walked on. A second policeman stopped him.

This policeman was invisible inside a Trubble-Bubble, a patrol car. The Trubble-Bubble silently glided alongside Brin. Its voice said, "Hi. You're Brin, aren't you? Got a minute?"

"Certainly," Brin said and gave the sign. The Trubble-Bubble flashed its answering sign, and its voice said, "Like to step inside?"

"No. I'm busy."

"Fine. Fine. Whatever you say. But your friends are worried about you."

"What friends?"

"A particular friend. Tello. Senior Tello. Very anxious to get in touch with you. Wants to see you.

"Sorry, I'm busy."

"Fine. Whatever you say. Sure you won't step inside?"

"I told you, I'm busy."

"Fine. Well, that's it, then."

The Sign of Politeness flashed again, and as Brin made his reply, the Trubble-Bubble swelled outward toward Brin. Suddenly its soft, jelly-glassy pickups were around Brin's body, locking his arms, making it impossible to move. Part of the Trubble-Bubble's skin turned inside out and Brin and the pickups were inside the Trubble-Bubble.

Brin struggled, but the pickups, so soft and smooth and gentle, held him in their firm jelly. He shouted, but his shouts of rage were smothered, and the Trubble-Bubble's voice kept saying, "Take it easy now, everything's fine."

The Trubble-Bubble silently and comfortably adjusted its shape and size to its new passenger, gently forcing Brin to sit. Brin shouted, "Let me out!" The policeman's voice said, "Shut your mouth," and his elbow slammed into Brin's ribs.

The pain was unexpected, but not as unexpected as the realization of what was being done to him. For the second time in one day, Brin was being beaten down—taught his place. And his body was heaving, shaking and making noises. He was crying, actually crying.

In a hidden underground part of the center, the Trubble-Bubble ejected Brin right at Tello's feet. "Hello, hello!" said Tello, smiling. *"What* a day you're having, Brin!"

Brin had to let Tello help him to the elevator.

"You can't do this!" Brin shouted. "How dare you!"

"Speak when you're spoken to, remember?" Tello said, smiling. But Brin could sense the man's anger. The walls of the hot little room seemed to totter and sway, pressing in on him. It was unbelievable. The world had gone mad and now the madness was smiling at him, almost laughing at him, with perfect white teeth.

"Open that door," he told Tello. "I'm leaving!"

"Do as you're bid," Tello grinned.

Madi came in and Brin turned to her. "Help me!" he demanded. "Make Tello let me go! Stop him from being rude!"

She stared at him without expression, then said to Tello, "He just won't *learn*, will he? With his IQ, you'd think he'd be able to *learn.*"

"Learn what?" Tello prompted, laughing softly.

"Learn to do what he's told. Learn how unimportant he is. Learn that he's just a stupid kid who's got to obey his elders."

"He'll learn," Tello said, still laughing. Then his big hand darted out and seized Brin's chin. Brin could feel his lips twist into a ridiculous shape and heard the absurd protesting noise the hand forced out of his mouth.

"Listen and learn, Brin." Tello wagged Brin's head with his big hand. "Listen and learn, right?"

Brin made a strangled sound. The big hand hurt. So did the suspicion that Tello was enjoying himself.

"You're merely part of an experiment, Brin. Just a little part of a big experiment. The experiment will go on and on until it succeeds. It will go on with or without you, Brin."

Tello set Brin free, then settled back in his chair.

"You don't matter, the experiment matters, do you understand? Brin doesn't matter, but the Reborns matter. We can always get another Brin, but we can't easily replace Brian and Mavis and Mrs. Mossop. Clear so far?"

Brin mumbled. Madi said, "Answer Senior Tello properly!"

Brin said, "Clear . . ."

"The Seniors aren't pleased with me," said Tello. "The experiment isn't going well enough or fast enough."

"That's not *my* fault!" Brin burst out.

"There you go again," Tello said, "thinking of yourself! *You* don't matter!—unless you *interfere* with the experiment—"

"By interrupting it," Madi said. "By feeling sympathy. Or by taking sides with the Reborns against what you call 'injustice' or 'unkindness.'"

Tello held up a hand to silence her. "Or by doing anything except what we tell you to do. We don't want your opinions about our policies and actions. We want only your obedience. Clear?"

Madi flicked Brin's shoulder with the back of her hand. "Answer Senior Tello!" she said.

"I understand," Brin muttered.

"He understands," Tello said, grinning at Madi. "And he's going to be a good boy from now on, isn't that right, Brin?"

"Particularly this evening," Madi said. "He's going to be a very good boy this evening."

"So he is, so he is," Tello said. "Because this evening is important. This evening we intend to apply a bit more pressure—"

"Pressure?" Brin said. He saw in his mind's eye the faces of the Reborns—Mavis making soldier's toast, Mrs. Mossop banging down the iron, Brian polishing the shoes; the time when Mavis cut her knee. He saw the inefficiency and grubbiness of their world, as well as its warmth and hidden strength—a warmth and strength that had no place in his world.

"A bit more pressure," Tello said. "Quite a bit more." Was he enjoying himself, Brin wondered; or was he forcing himself to "act tough." Tello stood up and stretched. Madi bit her lower lip.

"What's going to happen this evening?" asked Brin.

Tello stopped stretching and said, "Mrs. Mossop."

"What about her? What are you doing to her?"

"Writing her out of the scenario. We don't need her anymore."

Brin felt his mouth go dry.

"We're killing her off," Madi said, resting her slim brown hand on her knee.

"What do you mean? You can't mean—"

"Killing her off. She gets an electric shock from that switch she uses to turn on her ironing light. The shock kills her. We've boosted the current." Madi's fingers stroked her rounded knee.

"But why? *Why?*"

"Don't need her. I told you. We want to see how the children react to her loss, to coping by themselves."

"But I can't see *why* . . ." Brin's voice failed him.

Madi, suddenly furious, jumped to her feet. "Oh, for heaven's *sake!*" she shouted. "He's so dumb!"

Tello waved her aside. "Brin, I've told you before, but I'll tell you again for the last time. *Sleepers,* Brin. Our civilization runs on Sleepers. We don't fight because we don't want to, but it's because of Sleepers. We don't commit crimes because of Sleepers. We've got communities, societies, nations—a whole world—that lives in peace and prosperity because of Sleepers."

"I know all that," Brin said. "But why can't you simply make Reborns and give them Sleepers? Why must you hurt them—"

Madi, her voice still filled with a disgusted boredom, said, "Our generation is about the fifth Sleeper generation. The early generations resisted Sleepers. There were outlaws, renegades, rebels—people who *resisted* Sleepers—until quite recently. Who told you Sleepers are infallible? Who knows how well Sleepers will work on early generations of Reborns?"

Brin thought, "I suppose she's right. I don't know. . . ." His mind whirled. His armpit itched.

Tello's voice stopped him thinking further. The Senior said, "Sleepers aren't a cure-all—an instant remedy. It's taken generations to develop—with the aid of Sleepers—the people of our world. Even today we get our failures and throwbacks . . . people who revolt, who use violence, who defy society. We don't talk about them. We hide them. We call them dissidents. It's a nice soft word. . . ."

"Your precious Reborns," Madi said, "could be incurable dissidents."

"But you haven't even tried Sleepers on them!" Brin said.

"We condition them," said Madi. Not too much, but enough. We let them remember some things—let them have thoughts to build on—thoughts about you and Uncle Rick. We condition them for safety: to keep them in the scenario. It could take years—lifetimes—generations—to know if complete Sleepering is possible."

"And now," Tello said, "all we can do is measure their

difference from us by testing them to the limit. Putting them to the sort of test that invites a dramatic, even violent, response."

"And they will take a violent test this evening," Madi said.

"You will help, Brin," said Tello. "You won't hinder. Understand?"

"I will help," Brin muttered. For the third time that day, he felt tears in his eyes.

The evening started in the same old way. Brian throwing his book bag in the corner, Mavis making him pick it up. Playing ludo, bickering about who should make the tea. "I made it last time!" "You didn't!" "I did!" "Well, I'll do it when I've won this game." "Fat chance! Come on, six. I want another six. . . ."

Mavis threw a six, chuckled, and put out her last man. She already had two home. Brian scowled, threw a two, and groaned. One of Brin's men was right behind him, only three squares away. "Three! Three!" Brin prayed. "Three! *Please!*" he cried. For the moment, the game had carried him away. He threw the dice, got a four and beat the floor with his fists while Brian shouted, "Ha-*ha!* Ha-*ha!* One step behind you! Just you wait!"

Then Mrs. Mossop came in. "Well, that's one way to win the war, I suppose. *Ludo*, at *your* age!" She sniffed, and dumped her carrying bag on the ironing board. "They caught it down by the firehouse last night. What a mess, the bank's got all its windows broke," she said. "Pity the

Germans didn't blow the safe open, I'd have bought a ticket for that. . . . And no tea, you haven't even put the pot to warm, well, I *must* say!"

She began her high, weak singing. Brin tried not to see the old gypsylike face or hear her singing. He did not even notice when Brian threw a one, yelled "Whoopee!" and swept his man off the ludo board. He felt the white chill of despair invade him.

Mavis noticed. "You all right?" she said. "You look funny. . . ."

"He's broken-hearted!" Brian said. "I've sent him home again!" And he slammed Brin's man back into its starting place. "Now I'm going to get you, Mave!" he chuckled.

"Are you all right?" Mavis asked again.

"I was just—just thinking."

"Thinking about what?" Mavis insisted.

"Oh, come on, let's play if we're going to play!" Brian said, shaking the dice.

"Just thinking. Thinking about nothing, really," Brin said. He glanced sideways at Mrs. Mossop. She was not yet ready to start ironing: she was getting cups and saucers out and peering into the tin box with the pictures of King George V and Queen Mary on its sides.

"Were you thinking about *him?*" Mavis leaned forward. "About your Uncle Rick?"

"Yes," Brin lied. "I was wishing he'd turn up."

"It's your turn!" Brian said, crossly. But Mavis was hardly listening. Automatically, she threw the dice—a six; threw again—a four; and put her last man home. "What rotten luck!" Brian shouted, furious. "First a six, and then a four! Honestly!"

"Uncle Rick has to come to England sometime, doesn't he?" Mavis said, her face close to Brin's. "They have conversion courses, don't they—you know, to learn to fly new planes and things like that. So he's got to come here sometime, doesn't he?"

Mrs. Mossop poured the tea, singing "Sally, Sally, born in our alley."

Brin said, "Oh yes, he's coming over. He must. You saw his letter, he said he was coming over but didn't know when."

Mrs. Mossop put her two irons down by the kitchen stove.

They drank their tea. "He'll get leave, of course," Mavis said. "He probably won't," Brian said spitefully, still angry about Mavis's luck with the dice. "He might not get leave at all. Don't you know there's a war on?"

Mrs. Mossop went to the irons, picked one up and held it close to her cheek to test the heat. She put the iron back in front of the coals. Not hot enough.

Mavis, squatting on the floor in front of the kitchen stove, had her chin in her hands. She stared into the fire, then into Brin's eyes. "If only!" she said, "if only he'd come! I think about him all the time. I wish and wish and wish! I . . . *concentrate* on making him come—on hearing his footsteps in the passage outside, then his hand knocking on the door, and his voice calling out!" Her fists were clenched, her eyes wide.

Brian said, "That's funny," and Brin thought he was going to make a nasty remark. But he didn't. Instead, he said, "I do the same thing. I concentrate on him coming .... You know, imagining his face—I mean, we've seen the photographs ... and wishing he'd appear."

He paused and said, "It's so dull! The war and the blackout and everything. I thought the war would be exciting, but we seem to spend our whole lives in this moldy old kitchen. I wish he'd come! Why doesn't he come?"

Mrs. Mossop sang, "Some Day My Prince Will Come," but Mavis and Brian ignored her. Brin stared at them, anxious and guilty.

"Them irons ought to be ready by now," said Mrs. Mossop. She reached out to switch on the light over the ironing board.

"Wait!" shouted Brin, his voice almost a scream.

Brian, jerked out of his dream, said, "What? Wait for what?"

Mavis said, "What's wrong? What are you shouting for?"

Brin muttered, "Sorry. I thought I heard something. Something outside."

"Uncle Rick?" Mavis breathed.

"Uncle Rick?" Brian said, his eyes fixed on the door.

"Uncle Rick," Mrs. Mossop said, shaking her head. "You and that uncle of yours. . . ." Again she reached out her hand to the switch.

Before Brin could act—before another word could be spoken—there was a knock on the kitchen door. A young man's voice called, "Hey! It's pitch-dark out here—hey, anyone home?"

Mavis flew to the door and opened it.

Framed in the doorway, tall and smiling, stood Uncle Rick.

It was impossible, but it was true. Uncle Rick was real. His big bushy moustache, as wide as the young, jolly face, was real. The worn blue RAF uniform, with its medal ribbons on the tunic, was real. The spotted scarf, the brown eyes—they were all real.

"Hello, kids!" said Uncle Rick. "Let's go out and paint the town red!"

Mavis ran to him and flung her arms around his waist, almost crying with pleasure.

Brian said, *"You're him!"* and stared. Then, remembering his manners, he silently held out his hand, unable to speak.

Brin hung back, not knowing what to think or say: the only word in his mind was, "Impossible!"

"Shake hands with your uncle, Brin!" said Rick. Brin, uncertainly, took the man's hand. It was a solid, flesh-and-blood hand. It gripped Brin's hand strongly.

"You're Mrs. Mossop!" cried Uncle Rick, and he strode across the floor to shake her hand. She changed, before their eyes, into a flirtatious young woman. "Ooh!" she said. "A pleasure, I'm sure!" She dabbed at the hair over her ears.

"Well, where are we off to?" said Uncle Rick.

"Out!" Mavis said. "Anywhere, but *out!* Out of here! Take us out, Uncle Rick!"

"No!" Brin said, but nobody listened to him, nobody heard.

"Let's go!" said Uncle Rick.

"I must change," Mavis began, but Uncle Rick picked her up, whirled her around on his arm and said, "No time! You look wonderful."

Mavis and Brian ran around in circles, changing shoes, running combs through hair, pulling collars straight, chattering with delight. Brin tried to imitate their enthusiasm while his mind raced. Mrs. Mossop nodded and beamed, beamed and nodded. "You're never going out like that, young lady!" she told Mavis. "Your hair's like a rat's nest." She dabbed at Mavis with a comb, while Mavis hopped up and down and cried, "Hurry! Let's go! Let's get *out!*"

Brin found himself at the door of the kitchen, trying to think of something—anything—to postpone the moment when the door opened to limbo, nothingness; and the scenario fell apart; and Madi and Tello stepped in with—with what? With fire, an explosion, nerve gas? "Just a minute!" he said, feebly. "What about Mrs. Mossop?"

"She's coming too!" Uncle Rick smiled.

"But we can't leave the house—"

"Can't take it with us, either!" Uncle Rick said, laughing.

"The blackout," Brin said, hopelessly.

"Come *on,*" Brian said. "Paint the town red! Let's go!"

"Look out, London, we're on our way!" shouted Uncle Rick.

He turned the worn brass handle of the kitchen door and led the way out.

They stepped from the kitchen into nothingness. Their footsteps and cheerful cries raised no echoes.

Holding hands, they stumbled on—"It's dark!"—"Who was worrying about the blackout, Brin?"—"Oooh! It's spooky!"—and giggled and blundered and tripped their way toward a faint light ahead of them

"Front door, where are you!" called Uncle Rick. Then, "Funny sort of door, doesn't seem to want to open!—No, wait—ah! Gotcha!" Suddenly the five of them were in light that shifted and winked and glared, blinding light.

They were in a street of the city that only Brin knew.

"But it's not possible!" Mavis gasped, staring at the whirling lights, the glare, the glassy towers.

"I don't understand!" Brian muttered.

"What price the blackout?" Uncle Rick muttered.

"That pavement's moving, it's moving all by itself!" said Mrs. Mossop. More than any of them, she looked out of place in the city of the future: the colored lights of the city painted her worn old face and clothes a hundred shifting colors, none of them right.

Brin kept quiet. There was nothing he could say or do. He could only wait for *them* to take action: to do something to remove Mavis, Brian, Mrs. Mossop and Uncle Rick. They were in the wrong time, the wrong place. They *looked* wrong (but so far, not one of the busy people passing by had looked their way! It was rude to stare, thank goodness). But surely one of Brin's party would soon start asking unanswerable questions about the clothes worn by the people of the city, the lights, the structures, the words and pictures on the signs.

It was Uncle Rick who supplied an answer to the impossible. To Brin's astonishment, Uncle Rick began to chuckle. "Well, *well!* This beats everything! I've *heard* of places like this, but never thought I'd live to see one!"

"Places like what?" Brin said.

"Dummy targets!" said Uncle Rick, still chuckling. "Big spoofs! But on this scale!"

"What do you mean?" Mavis asked, skipping along beside him, her arm through his.

"Keep moving!" Uncle Rick said. "Keep walking! I want to see this—and I don't want to be picked up by the MP's!"

Now they were following Uncle Rick, walking briskly among the people of the city. Still nobody looked at them. The very drabness of their clothes provided some sort of concealment. "MP's?" Brian said. "I don't understand—"

"Military police!" Uncle Rick told him. "Keep walking! Don't look so surprised, try to look normal! Don't you see, we're not supposed to be here—not supposed to know such a place exists! We could be picked up at any moment! But I must see it all!"

"Dummy target, you said dummy target!" Brian insisted. "What did you mean?"

Uncle Rick's voice was excited but low as he explained.

"Dummy targets! To fool the old Germans, don't you see?" he said. "They come over with their bombers to hit London or another big city—can't find it always, because of the blackout—get confused, don't know where they are—then suddenly see all these *lights!* So what does the old enemy think?"

"I don't know, I don't understand—" Mavis said.

"He thinks he's over a neutral country!" Uncle Rick hissed, unable to keep himself from grinning at the cleverness of it all. "Thinks he's over Sweden or Switzerland—anywhere. Anywhere but England! All these lights, just like peacetime—poor old Germans think a gremlin's got at their navigational aids, or the navigator of the plane has gone crazy and the whole operation's gone west—so he radios back to base, and we intercept the radio calls and our fighters are waiting!" He began laughing out loud, then stopped.

"Up there!" he said, quietly. "No, don't stop walking, and don't stare—but look up there! On top of that building!" They looked and saw strange aerials and delicate grids spouting from a skyscraper. Brin knew they were climate-control sensors, part of the system that controlled the climate of the sealed city. But Uncle Rick said, "Some sort of radio-beam disorter, to mess up all the German signals, I suppose that's it—make their navigational equipment give false information, make them think they're hundreds of miles off target!" He whistled admiringly and said, "But a whole city! A thing on this scale! All these people working on it, living in it! And we used to think the Nazi scientists were hot stuff!"

Brin listened to Uncle Rick's words with anxiety and fear. The Seniors would do something, soon. What? His left armpit itched savagely. Why? His mind flickered and changed like the lights of the city.

Above the heads of the crowd he could see the smooth, domed top of a Trubble-Bubble. "Uncle Rick!" he said, warningly, but Uncle Rick would not pay attention to him: he was talking about decoy raids, mock attacks and all the tricks opposing air forces played on each other. Brian and Mavis hung on his words. Mrs. Mossop hurried along behind, her feet tired and her face set with the effort of keeping up.

The Trubble-Bubble silently eased toward them.

"Uncle Rick!" Brin said, pulling at the man's arm. But it was too late. The Trubble-Bubble was alongside them now, and its voice cleared its throat and spoke. "Hello," it said, "everything all right?"

Uncle Rick said, "What—?" and stopped, his face frozen.

"Everything all right?" said the Trubble-Bubble.

Uncle Rick whispered, "The MP's?" then he answered the Trubble-Bubble. "Everything is fine! Carry on." To Brin he whispered, "Weird sort of wagon. Where does its voice come from?"

"Carry on," repeated the Trubble-Bubble flatly. It did not change shape and extends its pickups as Brin feared it would. People glanced at the Bubble and the people around it and looked away, not wanting to get involved.

The Trubble-Bubble repeated, "Carry on," then, "Well, then, everything's fine. Have a good time." But it did not move away.

"Lots of things happening tonight," it said. "Music in the center. Athletics meet, too. Lots of things to do and see." It was marking time, talking for the sake of talking. Brin knew the policemen inside were making their report, getting their instructions—

A flock of pedalec riders came weaving through the crowds. Silvery bells jingled. "Hello," said the Trubble-Bubble, "citizens having fun! Make way for them! That's the way—"

And very softly, as Uncle Rick and the others moved back, the Trubble-Bubble added, "Not you, Brin. Come here."

The pedalecs glittered and whirred past, cutting off Brin from the others. "Yes?" he said to the Trubble-Bubble.

"Orders for you. Orders from above. Get them back. Take those people back to the scenario. Those are your orders. You understand?"

"Yes."

"Do it now. Don't waste time. We'll be watching. They'll be watching. Better obey, and fast."

"All right."

"For your own good," the Trubble-Bubble said, and it glided away.

Brin stood still, trying to think. "For your own good"— perhaps. But for their good? Would it be good for them to take them back to the scenario?

Brian said, "What was that thing saying to you?"

"Nothing. Just talking about the entertainments," Brin said, still trying to think.

Brian said, "What a super car! What a super place!" He looked about him excitedly. "What was that about entertainments?" he said.

"Entertainments?" said Uncle Rick. "Good idea! Let's go places and do things! Where shall we go? The athletics? The music? What do you prefer?"

Brin thought, "Yes—let's go somewhere. Anywhere. The Seniors can't hurt us while we're all together, out in the open, among the people. But once we're alone, back in the scenario, they've got us where they want us—"

"Athletics!" Brian said.

"No, music!" said Mavis.

"How do you vote, Mrs. Mossop?" Uncle Rick said.

"I like music," she said, "if it's nice music. I like nice music." She was out of place and she knew it. Worse, she was suspicious. She was looking hard at the strangely dressed people of the strange, scintillating, light-flooded world.

"Brin?" said Uncle Rick. "What's your vote?"

"Athletics," Brin said.

"So I've got the casting vote," Uncle Rick said, smiling. "It's up to me. Right. Tell you what we'll do—we'll go to both!"

Mavis danced around him, saying, "Yes! Super! Both! Athletics first, then the music. Or the other way around. I don't care! But let's do both!"

"All right, Mrs. Mossop?" Uncle Rick asked.

"A nice cup of tea," she said. "That's what I could do with. . . ."

"A nice cup of tea!" Brin thought. "I wonder what she'd make of our drinks, and the places we drink them?" Aloud he said, "They'll have tea at the sports place, won't they? They're bound to have a café or restaurant—"

To himself he thought, "Yes, the Sports Center. That would be the safest. Fewer people, all those activity rooms and changing rooms and corridors and walkways. . . . We could get lost in the Sports Center."

Aloud he said, "Uncle Rick, I know where the Sports Center is! Let's go!"

Uncle Rick stared at Brin, puzzled. "Come off it, old boy! How could you know?"

"I—I saw a sign," Brin said. "It pointed that way. . . ." To avoid explanations, he began to walk away and they followed him. He avoided the moving walkways, knowing that the Trubble-Bubbles would spot them most easily there. He wove through the crowds, choosing the places where the bright lights cast their darkest shadows.

The others seemed happy to follow his lead. Brin heard Uncle Rick's cheerful voice telling Mavis and Brian, "I was knocked for a loop when that thing came along! Thought it was the MP's! Mind you, I've got my leave pass—everything in order—but you never know. I could be recalled at a moment's notice. After all, there's a war on. Though you'd hardly know it, looking at this place. . . ."

They reached the Sports Center and Brin suddenly remembered the girl at the entrance. She or someone like
her would be there, to check ID bands. But then he remembered a side exit. Did the door work only one way?
He gulped and pushed the door. It opened and they
pushed through, Uncle Rick still talking, Mavis still
hanging on his arm, her laughing face turned to him,
Brian still wide-eyed and ready for anything.

"Are you sure we can get a cup of tea here?" Mrs. Mossop looked anxiously at the fused-glass walls, the silently
moving stairs of the escalators, the luminous panels of
light. "Doesn't look like the sort of place that would serve
tea. . . ."

Brin forced energy into his voice and movements.
"Come on, come on!" he shouted. "Follow me! Come on,
Mrs. Mossop!"

He pushed her onto an escalator. It took them up, as he
knew it would, to the long, blank corridors encircling the
center. Passages and doorways led off to the various activi-
ties, each labeled with a lit sign. Brin did not want them
to look too closely—to see the strangeness of everything.
He almost ran down the empty corridors, making the rest
keep up with him. "Tea!" he shouted. "Nice cup of tea for
Mrs. Mossop! Whoopee!" He clowned and waved his
arms, feeling his left armpit itch.

He managed to break away from the rest completely,
running well ahead, jumping in the air and bringing his
heels together, yodeling and whooping, behaving like a
happy madman. He wanted to get to a refreshments

room—an empty one. He had to make sure it was empty before the others caught up with him.

He pushed open the door of the same room he had used when he last visited the Sports Center. He looked inside. Warm, soft lights, soft seats, clean and welcoming—and it was empty! They were safe. Safe for minutes, a half hour, even an hour!

"Come on!" he called, over his shoulder. "In here! It's great! Come in here!"

Smiling, chattering and joking, they entered. "I'll get drinks and things!" Brin said, and turned his back on them so no one could see the terror on his face.

Soon, he knew, someone would say, "Don't you need some money?"—but money was obsolete.

Soon Mrs. Mossop would say, "Oh, I don't like *that,* are you sure they don't have a nice cup of tea?" Tea was obsolete too.

Soon the screens on the walls would light with advertisements, news summaries, entertainment flashes—all of them alien, all impossible to explain, all belonging to a time years ahead of their time. . . .

It was hopeless, but he had to go on with the play. He pressed buttons at the automatic serving center. Frujuice, Fiz, Chocmalt . . . the beautiful, colorful, hygienic, disposable beakers nestled in hygienic and colorful trays. "And a Kolamint!" cooed the recording from the automatic dispenser. Fortunately they were talking too loud to hear the voice. Brin knew Uncle Rick would no doubt offer money to pay when he brought the drinks to the table. He would have to take the coins and pretend to feed them into the machine.

But Mrs. Mossop would still want a cup of tea. . . .

He began to carry the loaded tray—remembering just in time not to put it on the Choot, the automatic delivery system—to the table. His hands shook and the liquids jiggled in their beakers.

As he reached the table, a door at the other end of the room opened and closed silently. A girl came in. Brin could make out her long hair and long bare legs. The whiteness of her brief sports outfit was almost luminous in the shaded warm light. Brin could not see her face, it could be anyone. It could even be Madi!

He knew it was Madi when he saw the girl begin to make the Sign of Politeness—then check herself. She turned the sign into a vague wave of the hand. She murmured a vague, friendly sound of greeting.

Brin put the tray down. Another moment and the drinks would have spilled: his hands were shaking.

Madi came closer. Brin cursed her silently. Uncle Rick stared at her legs and whistled softly. Brin saw his teeth gleaming as he smiled under his big, wispy moustache.

Madi walked past them to the pressed buttons. Now her back was to Brin and the others. Brin felt he was choking. Madi had found them. No doubt Tello and the other Seniors also knew where he was. The Trubble-Bubbles were outside, waiting. Brin knew it would not be long before it was all over.

Mrs. Mossop nervously sipped her drink. "It's very nice,

I'm sure, but you'd have thought they'd have tea. . . ."
Uncle Rick tried not to stare at Madi. Mavis and Brian,
silent for a moment when Madi came in, were talking
again—"Mine's super, like an orange and lemon and
pineapple all mixed up!"—"Let's swap, you have a sip of
mine, I'll have a sip of yours!"—"Only a sip, no gulping!"

A screen on the wall lit up. The usual mellow little
chimes sounded, politely. A written message appeared on
the screen:

ATENSHUN PLEAZ!

Madi turned, smiled and called, "I think you've left one
of your drinks behind. . . . Would someone like to come
and get it?"

Uncle Rick began to get up from his seat, but Brin
muttered, "No, I'll do it. My fault." He went over to
Madi. The screens now flashed the word:

URJENT!

Brian giggled and said, "Can't spell!"

Brin stood by Madi. His voice would hardly work.
"Yes?" he croaked.

She smiled and held out a drink to Brin. Speaking
loudly enough to be overheard, she said, "This drink isn't
mine, so I suppose it must be yours." She smiled again and
continued, speaking very softly, "You were told to get
them back to the scenario. You didn't do it. All right. Now
you can have it either way—nice or nasty. The nice way is
to get them back—"

"But I can't just—they haven't finished their drinks—I've no reason to make them go—" Brin said.

"We've thought of that. Watch the screens."

The screens now displayed:

> URJENT!
>
> LEEV THE SENTER!
>
> UNEXPLODED BOM

Even as Brin watched, the spelling changed:

> URGENT!
>
> LEAVE THE CENTER!
>
> UNEXPLODED BOMB

The screen began to flash the message. The chimes sounded continuously, urgently.

"The nice way is to get them back," Madi repeated. "Do it any way you like. We have a taxi outside. Get them into it."

"And the nasty way?" Brin said. "No, don't tell me. You'd destroy them here, wouldn't you? Kill them in front of each other?"

"We wouldn't do it noisily," Madi said, smiling brightly. "But we'd do it. We'd start with Mrs. Mossop. She should be dead by now anyway."

Brin said, "All right. I'll get them back to the scenario."

"It's a blue taxi with a white stripe," said Madi.

The screens said:

> LEAVE THE BUILDING
>
> IMMEDIATELY
>
> TRANSPORT IS PROVIDED

Brin rejoined his party. "Rotten shame!" Mavis said gulping down her drink as she stood up.

"The Germans ruin everything," Brian grumbled.

"Better get out, and quickly," Uncle Rick said, helping Mrs. Mossop to her feet. To Brin he said, "Lead on!"

Brin led them along the corridors, through the exit door, to the street. A blue taxi with a white stripe slid like a fish toward them. "In you get!" said the driver. "Can't tell when that bomb might go off!"

Before Brin could prevent it, Uncle Rick had bundled him and the others inside the cab.

Minutes later, they fumbled their way through the dark place that represented the hall of the old house: they were back in 1940, back in the kitchen, back in the scenario.

Trapped.

"I don't care!" Mavis said. Her eyes still sparkled, particularly when she looked at Uncle Rick. She whirled about the kitchen and scullery, filling a kettle, getting milk from the icebox, putting out cups and saucers—yet somehow wherever she was, she always seemed near Uncle Rick.

"*I* care!" Brian said. "Rotten luck! Especially for Uncle Rick. Just when we had found that terrific place—and everything set for a terrific evening—that's when the stupid rotten *war* has to come in and spoil everything!"

"I don't care!" Uncle Rick said. "Stop moaning! Here we are together, and I've got forty-eight hours' leave, and the kettle's on—and I've met Mavis and Brian and Mrs. Mossop for the first time . . . and seen my nephew Brin once again—so are we downhearted?"

He cocked a hand comically behind his ear to receive the answer: *"No-o-o!"* Brian and Mavis shouted their "No!" lustily. Mrs. Mossop giggled her "No!" then said, "Tsk, tsk," and needlessly rearranged all the cups and saucers, smiling to herself. When Uncle Rick called her the Good Fairy of the Teapot she said, "Oh, go along with you," and pushed his shoulder with her hand. Her glasses seemed to twinkle.

Brin was silent: he knew. Not everything, but more than enough. He knew that some sort of curtain was to descend over the scenario. There had to be an ending—most probably a violent ending. He wondered why he was not more afraid.

He knew that Uncle Rick, now the central figure of the play, was an impossible lie. He could not exist, yet . . . "Ludo!" Uncle Rick shouted. "Haven't played it for a hundred years! Ludo! Imagine! When I was a kid, I always played red."

"You can be red now," Mavis said. "Here you are!" She twisted the board around on the carpet in front of the kitchen stove so that the red base faced Uncle Rick. "I don't mind what color I am," she said.

"But you'll have to take green!" Brian said. "You hate being green!"

"No I don't. I *like* green." She put Uncle Rick's pieces in place for him.

He said, "Right! Just watch me! Just watch me, that's all! Six after six! Never fails! King of the six-shooters, that's your Uncle Rick!"

Brin slowly set out his yellow pieces and made himself

remember the scene around him. The kitchen stove, with its name ALBION on the oven door and the words PEACE & PLENTY below, in smaller cast-iron letters. The smell of the stove's glowing coals, and its private clinkings and tickings and sudden minor landslides. The kettle, heating now, singing to itself. The faded, ugly pattern of the carpet on which he knelt, with its little black-brown holes made by burning fragments of coal. The creaking of the wicker chair, where Mrs. Mossop sat, knitting, her face creased and shining. The familiar ugliness of the kitchen, with the blackout curtains like a big wall over the main window. Blackie, half asleep on Mavis's school scarf, which she had thrown on the lid of the icebox. Worn linoleum, chipped chairs, oilcloth and ironing, dust on the cord from which hung the glaring electric-light bulb in the middle of the ceiling. The sparkle of the cups, the smell of the tea.

All to go soon, he knew. How soon? How would the end come?

"Six!" yelled Brian. "One!—two!—three!—four!—five!—six! And *another* throw, *if* you please! . . . One, two, three, four. . . . And that gets me safely home, thank you very much! Beat that, Uncle Rick!"

"Enough of this!" Uncle Rick growled. "Give me that dice." He rolled his eyes and shook the dice in his clenched fist, near to his ear. "Six!" he said to the dice. "You hear me? Six! Come on, come on, *come on*. . . ."

"Come on!" said the Senior Elect, impatiently. He tapped the horseshoe-shaped table with his old-fashioned ball-point pen. "We will have no more recriminations and postmortems and examinations of what has been done. I am asking you what *will* be done. Tello?"

Tello, his face troubled, said, "I think ... I think we must keep on with the experiment. We simply can't throw it all away."

The horse-faced Senior said, "Simply! He says, 'simply'! There is nothing simple about what is happening. It is complicated, difficult, even dangerous—"

"Dangerous?" said the Chinese Senior in her high, pleasant voice. "I do not see a danger. I see a mystery, but where is the danger?"

"The mystery is the danger," replied the horse-faced Senior.

"If there is a mystery," said the Senior Elect, tapping his pen faster, "will someone please explain it and solve it. If there is a danger, we will face it. But let us do it promptly!"

Tello sighed. "We are a scientific race," he began. "We rely on science to provide our needs and advance our purposes. The Reborn program is typical of our approach. Reborns are the scientific answer to a problem caused by a scientific disaster."

"Please, get on!" said the Senior Elect.

But Tello continued to speak slowly, almost tiredly. "From the moment we constructed the first Reborn, we became creators of life. We reached a godlike summit, through science. We knew what we did; we knew how we did it. We understood, completely, the nature of our achievement. ...

"But now we find that the creatures we created can do something more than us. Without science—without our huge store of knowledge, built up over the centuries—the creatures we made, mere Reborn children, have outdone us. They, too, have made a living creature! This Uncle Rick! . . .

"And they've made him from nothing! No genes, no chromosomes, no electric currents, no genetic recoders! They merely said, 'Let there be life!'—and there was life."

The Senior Elect rubbed his nose. "The purpose of this meeting is to decide what to do about this—Uncle Rick. Granted—he is scientifically impossible. Granted—his existence contradicts the basis of our whole civilization. So what *do* we do about him, and his creators?"

"Terminate their lives," said the horse-faced Senior.

"Terminate them?" said a quiet Senior—a man who seldom spoke, a quiet, small man, leader of the team that made the Reborns. "I don't think you mean what you say. Terminate? I'm not sure—"

"Why not kill them?" snapped the Senior Elect.

"I was going to say," said the quiet Senior, "that I'm not sure we *can* kill them. Oh, I know, we made them, so we should be able to terminate them. But this Uncle Rick: he may not *consent* to death. He may refuse to be killed by our sort of science!"

"He is flesh and blood," said the horse-faced Senior. "Flesh and blood can be destroyed."

"And a spirit?" said the quiet Senior. "Can we be sure of destroying spirits, too?"

The Chinese Senior said, "But this is absurd! Now we are talking of ghosts and myths and bogeymen! Surely if you kill the flesh-and-blood body, you kill the person!"

Speaking almost to himself, the quiet Senior said, "Donald Duck."

The Senior Elect sighed elaborately and said, "I beg your pardon? Did I understand you to say 'Donald Duck'?"

"Oh, and Charlie Chaplin," said the quiet Senior. "And so many others—the great names—Shakespeare and Dickens and Bach. I can't remember all of them off-hand. Hardly my field. Buddha, Muhammad, Jesus Christ . . ."

"If there is a point, please get to it," said the Senior Elect icily.

"The point? Well, it is obvious, surely. The centuries pass, yet these people are all alive. They still live, in a sense. Our children still laugh at Donald Duck, all these years after he was created—"

"The point!" shouted the Senior Elect.

"But he has come to the point," said Tello. "He's saying that the parts of a person that are *not* flesh and blood can live on indefinitely. As witness the founders of religions, the great artists—even Donald Duck, who was never flesh and blood, never anything more than a series of funny drawings. Yet there is a force of the spirit, a life force, that survives—"

"Where is the danger in that?" said the horse-faced Senior.

The quiet Senior replied, "Strength. Such forces are strong."

"We are strong! Our science is strong!" said the Chinese Senior.

"But also weak," said the quiet Senior. "It was our science, remember, that nearly put an end to our human race."

"But we created Reborns from science!"

Tello said, "And the Reborns created a raw, natural human being. Without science! How did they do it? That is the mystery. Will they continue to do it? That is the danger. For if their humans, who can breed, prove stronger and more effective than our infertile humans, one day there may be no place left for us on this planet!"

There was a long silence. The Senior Elect broke it by throwing down his ball-point pen on the shining surface of the great desk. "Enough!" he shouted. "I will tolerate no more of this! These arguments end where they begin and begin where they end! This talk of spirits and mysteries and threats!" His voice cracked and for a moment became an old man's quaverings. He clenched his hands, set his mouth and spoke again, quietly.

"We must act," he said. "Act now, on the facts. Fact: the Reborns have broken out of the scenario. Fact: they have created a being who, some of you seem to believe, might threaten our own future. Which leads to three simple, easily answered questions on which I demand your votes and decisions.

"First, the experiment. Shall it continue, or shall we end it?

"Second, the Reborns. If we decide to remove them from the experiment, do we permit them to continue to exist—or do we terminate them?

"Third, the creature the Reborns created—this Uncle Rick. Does he live or does he die? And please do not tell me," he said viciously to the quiet Senior, "that Rick cannot be killed, because I say he can. . . .

"Those are the questions on which you will vote. When I have your joint decision, it will be acted on immediately. Other matters—what to do with the Reborn children if you decide that they may live, and so on—will be decided in due course.

"But now you will vote, without further delay, on the three major questions. On those questions and those questions only."

The Senior Elect gave the Sign of Politeness. The Seniors responded, then placed their hands on the surface of the table. Under their fingertips lay two flat tablets, flush with the table. A minute pressure, an invisible movement of the muscles of a finger, was enough to press down one of the two tablets. For the fingers of the right hand, yes. For the fingers of the left, no.

"You all ready?" said the Senior Elect. There was a murmur of assent—then Tello said, "You have not mentioned the boy Brin! Surely we must decide about him, too?"

The Senior Elect raised his eyebrows. "I cannot see why," he said. "Surely he can wait? Isn't his a—a rather separate case?"

Tello opened his mouth but decided not to speak. He,

too, lowered his hands until they rested on the shining table, over the two neat, flat, fatal tablets.

"Superman!" Uncle Rick cried, shaking his head admiringly. "That's what you are, Brin! How does he do it?" he asked Mavis and Brian. "I mean, he wasn't even trying! Not with us at all! Throwing the dice any old way—yet there he is, home and dry, while I've still got two men stuck at base—"

"I've got three!" Mavis groaned. "Brin sent two of mine back, and Uncle Rick caught me just when I was getting this one home. . . ." She groaned dramatically and leaned toward Uncle Rick, who patted her head and grinned at her.

Brin forced himself to make the right sounds and faces. He'd won two games of ludo in a row, barely knowing he had been playing. "Superior talent," Brin said. "Greater intellect! I'm just smarter than anyone else in the world, that's why I win—"

"Smarter?" said Brian. "Luckier, you mean! Honestly, the way Brin managed to keep out of my way when I was right on his tail—it just wasn't natural!"

Brin thought, "Not natural? Not natural . . . smarter . . . greater intellect . . . Superman."

Did the words add up to something? His high IQ. His fantastic memory. Were they natural? And if they weren't, what was the connection between his superman status and his itching armpit? To hide his face and his thoughts, he poured himself more tea.

"You don't want to drink that," said Mrs. Mossop. "That's dishwater! If you want tea, make a fresh pot. We could all do with another cup."

"Quiet!" said Mavis as she held a hand to her ear. A long way away, the sirens started. "Air-raid warning!" Brian said, disgustedly. "We can't get out of here, now. We're stuck."

"That Hitler," said Mrs. Mossop. "Well, I suppose I'd better do the ironing, then."

Hoping Madi, who was behind the dresser, could hear, Brin said, "Don't go near that light by your table, Mrs. Mossop! I touched it tonight and it gave me a shock! It ought to be fixed!" To himself he thought, "They're going to kill us all one way or another, I suppose. But at least we can all go together."

"It should be fixed right away," said Uncle Rick. "Let's have a look!" He went to the switch and pulled a fountain pen out of his pocket. With the pen, he flicked the switch—

There was a blue flash and a deafening sound. The switch rocketed across the room and smashed to pieces on the kitchen range. Smoke came from the wall. "I don't believe it! . . . I don't believe it," Uncle Rick repeated in a stunned voice. He stared at the gnarled, melted stump he held in his hand; it was all that remained of his fountain pen.

Brin began to shake with a laughter that he couldn't control. Brian was shaking and heaving too. "But look at my fountain pen!" Uncle Rick said. "It's been written off!"

"Pen . . . written off!" Brian said. "That's funny, you know! Pen, written off!"

And then they were all laughing, Brin and Mavis and Brian and Mrs. Mossop, laughing uncontrollably. Uncle Rick, too. The kettle boiled over, Blackie the cat said, "Mrr-aow!" and they laughed and laughed and laughed.

Much nearer now, the sirens swooped and moaned. Brin's laughter actually hurt him, his sides ached and his mind said, "So that's it: we're to be destroyed in an air raid. Very soon now." But aloud he said—his words broken into meaningless sounds by the racking, choking, glorious laughter—"Satisfied, Madi? Happy now, Tello? Because I'm happy! I don't care anymore! You can't hurt any of us now!"

For the explosion had set off an instantaneous explosion in his own mind. In that crashing split second, he had suddenly realized the truth about himself, a truth so awful and fundamental that it, too, had to be laughed at. The truth included the discovery that his whole life had been a lie—and even that false life was shortly to end.

He knew now why his left armpit itched. And that small revelation made him laugh all the more helplessly as, above the sound of the sirens, the sullen, pulsing, mumble of the approaching bombers was heard.

Tello's expression was even blacker than his skin. "You cannot do this!" he shouted.

The Senior Elect flinched, but then steadied his gaze and looked back at Tello. "We can," he said. "We will."

"The votes are cast," said the Chinese Senior, her voice as light and charming as ever. But this time she averted her eyes when she spoke.

"It is savage—stupid—brutal—wasteful!" cried Tello, unconsciously echoing the words once used by Brin.

"It will be done," said the Senior Elect. "It is being done. The vote has been taken. They die."

The quiet Senior stood on his feet, his face gray. "*I* voted that they live!" he said. "Let it be known how *I* voted!"

"We are not interested," said the Senior Elect. "Indeed," he added scornfully, "we do not hear you. We *must* not hear you. The vote is always secret. We do not ask and must not know how any one Senior voted."

"I think you know how I voted," said Tello.

The quiet Senior looked despairingly at Tello, then sank back slowly into his seat. "It is not—not *scientific*," he complained.

"Cruel, stupid, wasteful, inhuman!" cried Tello, alone and defiant on the floor of the chamber.

"Inhuman?" said the Senior Elect. "Ah! With that word you make some sense. Inhuman, certainly. Mavis, a Reborn. Brian, a Reborn. Mrs. Mossop, a Reborn. Uncle Rick—well, let us say a figment of the imagination—an effort of will disguised as a human."

"And the boy Brin?" demanded Tello.

"Enough!" said the Senior Elect. "It is nearly time. Tomorrow we have serious business to discuss. The matter before us tonight will very shortly be completed. Over and done with, Tello. Never to be discussed again, you understand?"

He rose to his feet. The others—all but Tello—also arose. The Senior Elect made the Sign of Politeness. The others—all but Tello—responded. All but Tello left the Council Chamber of the Elect, their robes hissing gently on the pictured floor.

Tello stood alone.

The bombs, still distant, whistled down, whistling out of tune with each other as they hit their targets and shook the kitchen.

Brin saw Mrs. Mossop's face turn yellow: saw her bite her lower lip, then catch herself doing it and make herself stop. "That Hitler," she said. "I'd give him Hitler. . . ."

"A play, a recording, a stage set!" thought Brin. "If only I could tell them! Lies, lies! But they would not believe me. And it would not help them. And there isn't time."

The drone of the bombers was very near now. The unsynchronized motors growled, *"Rrrrum . . . rrrum . . . rrrum"* as if a huge coarse mill wheel were turning in the sky, grinding lives between broken teeth. Blackie laid his ears back and jumped smoothly from the top of the icebox, then burrowed into the gap beneath it. *"He* knows what's good for him!" said Mrs. Mossop.

"If only I could tell them it's all right," Brin thought.

"Tell them that nothing is real—not the bombers, nor anything else. But would it help?"

Suddenly nearby antiaircraft guns began firing. Mavis moved, without meaning to, toward Uncle Rick; then, self-conscious, moved away again. But he reached out a long arm and drew her to him so that her head was against his chest. "Don't desert a fellow!" he said. "I can't stand the sound. Get nervous even when someone sets off a firecracker! Need moral support! Did I tell you how I got my medal? Would you like to hear? Well, I'll tell you. . . ." He began a story about being frightened by a bang inside his aircraft. He talked without a pause, his arm around Mavis, protecting her, talking faster and faster, to hold her attention, shield her from fear.

Outside, there was a very loud whistling shriek, and a horrifying smash that made the kitchen vibrate. Dust leaked from the ceiling.

Uncle Rick ignored it. "I was so frightened by the bang that I jumped out of my skin!—went straight up, straight through my aircraft, right up into the sky!"

"What happened then?" Brian said, grinning as he flicked dust from his face.

"Well, there was this German, an Me 109, just above me. Somehow I grabbed his tailwheel! He had to fly with me hanging on behind—but the extra weight wasn't what he'd reckoned with, so he started looping the loop . . . loooooping the looooop!"

More bombs fell, a whole slew of them. Not so near this time. Streets away. But Brin saw the crack in the ceiling, over the dresser, zip and spread. A fine trickle of plaster dust became a steady stream. The room shook again. The trickle became thick and threatening.

"Table!" Brian muttered and pushed Mrs. Mossop under the ironing table. But Uncle Rick did not stop telling his story. Even as he pushed Mavis under the table he was talking and grinning.

The crack in the ceiling widened. The ceiling sagged in the corner, very slightly at first, but another bomb fell and the room shook again and the triangular corner of the ceiling hinged downward. Only the top of the high dresser kept it in position. No one else noticed. They were listening to Uncle Rick.

"... This Me 109 was going round and round like a pinwheel. So fast that the pilot busted his straps and went hurtling through the canopy! Centrifugal force, you see! Very powerful ..."

"*A Reborn!*" Brin thought. "*That's what I am! I should have guessed earlier. The itching should have told me. I wonder how long ago they made me? It can't have been long. Otherwise the pinpricks in my armpit would have healed more completely, they wouldn't still itch from being so new. Idiot, why didn't I guess? A Reborn, just like the others! No, but not like them. I wasn't made from the rags and bones of their time! I'm one of the people of today, my body is smaller, I belong to the new, sterile breed of superhumans. I suppose I was given a super Sleeper to make me super-intelligent, super-useful for the great experiment, super-everything. Now I'm super-seded, superfluous, superannuated. I'm a dead loss, or just about to become one. ...*"

Bombs began screaming. The screams were the loudest yet. Uncle Rick paused and looked up at the ceiling. There was sweat as well as dust on his forehead. Mavis clutched his arm—her hands were white and clawed— and said, "Go on, Uncle Rick! Go on!" He heard her above the screaming of the bombs. He turned his head to one side, waggled his moustache and continued, "So the Me 109 whipped right around, turned head over heels— and flung me off the tailwheel! And you'd never guess where I landed!" Now he had to shout.

"Go on!" she said—she, too, had to shout above the screaming of the bombs—"Don't stop! It's so funny!" Her face was filled with terror, and her fingers clasped his sleeve.

"So I landed *in the seat of the Me 109!*" shouted Uncle Rick triumphantly. "Flew it back to base, I did!" Uncle Rick seized Brin and flung him at the table. "Get under! Quick!"

The bomb's screaming was intolerably loud—Brin wanted it to land and explode and blow them all to smithereens, then it would all be over and finished—why did it have to take so long? Had they got the recordings wrong? The bombers were only a recording, none of it was real, only the ending would be real, the last explosions, the deaths—

There was no room under the table for Uncle Rick. He was squatting by the table, waving his arms, finishing his story, shouting it, bellowing it. "So I flew the German plane back to base and they gave me a medal!" he yelled

"Captured enemy aircraft single-handed! Brave Uncle Rick!"

"Yes!" Mavis shouted, reaching out an arm, curling it around his neck. "Oh yes, Uncle Rick!" Brian had taken Uncle Rick's other hand, holding it tightly, looking into his eyes, making himself smile. And Mrs. Mossop was trying to smile too, her lips were moving and her head nodding as if to say, "Yes, yes, yes!" And Uncle Rick was outside the table, yet holding them all together, smiling right through their eyes and getting inside them, telling them, "Yes!"

The bomb exploded.

The city quivered. Riders stopped their pedalecs and looked around them. "What was that?"

"I don't know. Sounded like an explosion."

"An explosion? But that's impossible. We don't have explosions. . . ."

"We do. Remember years ago, when that electric feeder went up? That was a bang."

"What's an electric feeder?"

"I don't know. Something to do with the city's power supply, I suppose. But it went up. Bang."

"Well, everything's quiet now."

The riders remounted their machines. A Trubble-Bubble glided by, its voice cozy and cheerful. "Everything's fine," it said. "Enjoy yourselves. Everything's fine."

The pedalec riders rode off. The night sky glittered with signs and colored reflections from the tall, glassy buildings. If you looked hard, you could see the stars of the firmament beyond the transparent dome that covered the city. But the stars were dim against the flashing signs and gleaming walls.

"The bomb has exploded!" said the Senior Elect as the Council Chamber of the Elect vibrated slightly.

"I know," said Tello, bitterly. "I felt the force of the explosion. So did *they*. Only they felt it more strongly."

The horse-faced woman Senior said, "Very well arranged. A well-contained explosion. We only felt a tremor. I think congratulations are in order." She nodded approvingly at the quiet Senior. He had arranged the explosion. He shook his head angrily and turned away from her.

"A mere tremor," said Tello. "And for *them,* an inferno: flesh torn from bones, blood turned to vapor, brains mashed to pulp. Oh yes! Congratulations are in order!"

The Senior Elect said, "That will do," and touched a button under the desk. A wall lit up with motion pictures. They showed the people in the streets of the city. Heads turned, eyes looked about, groups of puzzled people formed and dispersed, talking to each other, asking questions. But soon the groups broke up. Shoulders shrugged, mouths smiled. People went their way.

"They hardly noticed it," said the Chinese-looking Senior brightly. "But I suppose we ought to make a news announcement, all the same? Just to set everyone's mind at rest?"

"Oh yes," said the Senior Elect. "Say something. Anything will do. What did we say last time? When we had to
dispense with those agitators, those dissidents? It was some
time ago, I don't remember."

"Something about an electric feeder," said the Chinese
Senior, smiling.

"Well, use that again," said the Senior Elect. "Electric
feeder. By the way, what *is* an electric feeder?"

He looked inquiringly toward the quiet Senior; but
once again, there was no reply other than an angry turn of
the head.

The Senior Elect said, "Ah well. Yes, I think we may
congratulate ourselves. The matter is concluded. Ended."

Tello stared at the Senior Elect and raised an eyebrow.
"Ended?" he said. "Perhaps. . . ."

The bomb exploded.

To Brin, its fall had been an eternity of stretched split
seconds.

The explosion, too, was another eternity. He saw, as if
by a lightning flash, the dingy kitchen heave, lift itself up-
ward, and the glass of an electric lamp crinkle and col-
lapse—perhaps he even saw the white-hot filament dim
and die and its tiny spiderweb snap its threads (but yes, he
did see Mavis, her eyes wide to receive the beam of pure
will from Uncle Rick, the will to live).

He saw the walls shake and crack, and the dishes break
as if hit by invisible bullets. The shelves leaped from their
brackets and split apart, showing clean white wood under

the old paint (and yes, he saw Brian's eyes turn from Uncle Rick to Mrs. Mossop, who still had a forced smile printed on her face).

He saw the ceiling fall, the walls rush toward him, the chairs spinning. He saw the kitchen stove split, and the iron word ALBION flying toward him, smashing through the leg of the table (and yes, he saw Uncle Rick's face— no, it was his eyes, it was his eyes that mattered—sure and smiling and saying "Yes!").

He saw Blackie, eyes blazing, pink mouth open showing white, curved teeth.

He saw the ceiling and the wall smash down on the icebox: it bulged and splintered and flattened.

He saw white flames and purple flames, flying glass and spurting dust.

He saw his own flesh tear from his fingers. (But yes! He had been born of a rag, a bone, a hank of hair, and Uncle Rick's eyes told him that a Reborn could be reborn!)

He shouted, "LIVE!"—and died.

Madi, her pretty face sulky and withdrawn, said, "I don't know what you are talking about. *I* don't hear voices."

Tello laughed and said, "Perhaps I should exercise more."

She said, "Yes. Perhaps you should. *Voices!*" She walked away from the big black man, disliking him. Before—but before *what?*—she had liked him better than any of the other Seniors, liked his massiveness, his deep, easy voice, the feeling of security and certainty he gave people. Now he made her uneasy—even angry. Everything seemed somehow different, ever since—since *what?*

Annoyed with herself, annoyed with thoughts of Tello, she took the walkway and headed for the Sports Center. She tried to concentrate on the bustle around her, the people, the signs, the buildings. But all the time her uneasiness nagged her. She had been quite all right before—before *what?* Since *what?* "All right, I'll admit it," she told herself. "Before those Reborns. After those Reborns. But why worry about them? They're finished now."

As for this talk of voices, hearing voices . . . Nonsense! *"I* don't hear them!" she said, under her breath. A man next to her on the walkway said, "Excuse me?" and she replied, "Oh, nothing!" and smiled at him, still more annoyed with herself. Hearing voices! It was her own voice that had spoken just now.

She showed her ID band at the center, changed in the changing rooms, swam six lengths in the pool, plunging through the artificial salty waves. She felt better. She lay on her back in a corner where the waves were small and gentle and looked at the water spilling over her stomach. Much better! She thought, "I wonder why more citizens don't come here. It makes you feel alive—"

Very loudly in her ear, a voice from nowhere shouted, "LIVE!"

She swallowed water, floundered, left the pool and stood under a freshwater shower. She turned the water to cold and let it chill her. "Cold commonsense," she murmured. She had not heard a voice. The voice had not shouted, "LIVE!" She was not going to hear the voice again, just when she was falling asleep. It was all nonsense. A trick of the brain.

"Brain, Brian, Brin," her mind said.

"Nonsense!" she shouted and turned the shower water on full. The water roared at her, drowning any possibility of hearing the voices. . . .

In the Council Chamber of the Elect, the Senior Elect said, "Any other business?" His voice was tired. But so was his body. "You are an old man!" he told himself. "Soon you can resign your position as head of the Western Elect, and become a philosopher, a commentator, a distinguished observer, an historian. You deserve your retirement. What did Shakespeare's Othello say? 'I have done the state some service. . . .' Othello, Tello. Perhaps Tello will take my place when I resign. I wish I could like the idea of him sitting in this chair when I am dead—"

"LIVE!" shouted a voice from nowhere, a deafening voice.

The Senior Elect jumped—pulled himself together—and repeated, "Any other business?" He hardly heard the replies. He was hearing voices! Time for him to retire. . . .

The Chinese Senior, alone in her apartment, made herself tea. A luxury. A treat not known to other people. She, however, had chosen to preserve the old custom and something of the formality of the oriental ceremony connected with tea-making. Not like the Japanese, of course: that

was going too far. But the quiet, meditative, private ceremony of boiling the water . . . setting the beautiful china-
ware . . . handling the bamboo spoons . . . was pleasant.
Very pleasant. It put her into a frame of mind that, she
knew, belonged to her ancestors. It placed her in another
time in history, took her away from a too crowded present.
It conferred a sort of dignity and calm on an overcrowded
life—

"LIVE!" the voice shouted.

She flinched, but ignored the voice. She took the bamboo scoop between her finger and thumb and measured
out the fragile tea leaves. Then she carefully, gracefully
lifted the little flowered teapot to—

"Tally ho!" said a voice, a laughing, cheerful, young
man's voice. "Brewing up? Wish I could join you, I'm
thirsty! Perhaps I *will* be able to join you—I hope I'm not
butting in, didn't see you clearly, can't quite make things
out—"

The voice faded and she sighed. It was happening more
and more often nowadays, hearing the voices. She completed her tea ceremony, sat down on the long wide sofa
and made herself concentrate on the fragrance of the tea.
She turned down the lights so that the low, cool, orderly
living room was illuminated only by one warmly glowing
sphere. She sipped the tea.

In the shadows of the corner, something dark moved.
Two greenish-yellow glints, like eyes. She jerked upright,
almost spilling the tea. It moved again!

She rose to her feet and went to the dark corner. As she

had expected, there was nothing there. Nothing at all. She stood, small and neat and determined, inspecting the corner. She thought she heard a sound, a high sound, like the mewing of a cat.

She bent down and looked more intently into the corner—then she remembered a nearby light switch and switched on a lamp. Nothing, except dust.

Shocked, she moved from the corner and walked briskly to the service room, where she touched a tiny flat switch. A small lilac-colored machine nosed out of the wall and began to run around the floor. With her toe, she guided the machine to the dusty corner, where it sucked up dust.

"Wait!" she cried—but it was too late. Before she could stop it, the machine got to the print in the dust—

The paw marks of a cat.

The machine gobbled it up.

"Carried?" said the Senior Elect. "Good. Carried. We are agreed, then, by a majority vote, to continue with the Reborn program."

Tello tried to speak. The Senior Elect raised his hand and silenced him. "No, Senior Tello. I must forbid you. We know your views. You have put them forth forcefully and clearly. But the overriding consideration is the continuance of the human species—"

"No Reborns, no human race!" interrupted the horse-faced Senior.

"You know the risks," Tello said, "that is all I wanted to say. To remind you, yet again, of the risks."

"We know the risks of *not* continuing with the program," said the horse-faced Senior, as she folded her arms.

The quiet Senior spoke. "You won't listen to me, I suppose," he began, speaking so quietly that the horse-faced Senior said, "Can hardly hear you. Wish you'd speak up!"

The quiet Senior cleared his throat and continued, "As I say, you won't listen to me, but—are there any other voices you should listen to, do you think?"

"Other voices?" said the Seniors.

"Don't know what he's talking about!"

"What voices?"

"Has he been *hearing voices?* Well, well!"

The indignant chorus died down. The quiet Senior said, "You have answered my question. There are no other voices you need listen to. Of course not. I am perfectly satisfied. Thank you."

There was a blank silence. At last the Senior Elect said, "Yes. Well. Turning to the question of the Reborn program . . ."

"I hear you!" said Tello. His voice was a quiet, velvet rumble. His eyes were closed. He lay on his back in the dark. Outside his bedroom, the city was quiet. Yet he still could not hear the voices properly.

"Go on, go on!" he said to the blackness.

". . . Don't know where I am half the time!" said Uncle Rick's cheerful voice—but Tello could hear the underlying anxiety and doubt. ". . . Ought to rejoin my squadron, I suppose. But they did give me leave. Got another forty-eight hours left. Plenty of time to look up Brin, my nephew. Nice kid, they tell me. Trouble is, I don't really know London. And the blackout doesn't help. . . ."

The voice faded. "Go on!" muttered Tello. But the voice was gone.

Then Brin spoke. "My armpit itches! I know why. At least, I did know, but I've forgotten. Brian doesn't like losing at ludo, does he? You should have seen his face when I threw that third six!"

Tello lay waiting. Only his lips moved. "Come on," he whispered, "tell me! Come and tell me! I'm listening."

Suddenly Mavis said, very loudly, "Oh, Blackie! You are a devil, that's the last of the milk!"

"Go on!" said Tello, but all he could hear was the *thump-thump-thump* of an iron on an ironing board.

"Mrs. Mossop?" said Tello. But the voices were gone. He sighed, turned over on his side and eventually fell into an uneasy sleep, filled with wild and impossible dreams, and voices calling.